ACCIDENTAL FUGITIVES

Also by J. David Cox

OUR LIFE OFF THE GRID:
An Urban Couple Goes Feral

CHOOSING OFF THE GRID

ACCIDENTAL
FUGITIVES

The FBI's Most Wanted Seniors

J. DAVID COX & SALLY J. DAVIES

Issued in print and electronic formats:

ISBN 978-0-9940145-5-9 (Book)
ISBN 978-0-9940145-1-1 (eBook)

OTG Publishing
Box 53
Surge Narrows, British Columbia
Canada   V0P 1W0
coxdavies@gmail.com

Editor and Book Design: Sally J. Davies
Cover: Emily Robertson

For Leo

CHAPTER ONE — *Charlie*

It was a deceptively quiet day in the Sonoran Desert. I was in the back garden practicing on my friend Steve's AstroTurf putting green. Nance was in the house and I heard her as she went to answer a knock at the front door. There was a muffled shout, unsettling enough to make me head to the sliding glass door to check on her, putter in hand. I stepped inside to see a sketchy looking man peering into our bedroom.

"What the *hell* do you think you're doing?"

He abruptly swung towards me and I could see that he was holding a gun in his hand. Instinctively I swung the putter hard and fast. It connected with the side of his head making a sharp popping sound. I couldn't pull it back. It was stuck. He fell and so did his blue-gray .45 automatic. It was quite a shock. For both of us.

My assailant was down and Nance was nowhere in sight. I had no idea what was going on but I figured he wasn't alone—maybe someone else was out front. I picked up his gun. Now armed, I checked to make sure the safety was off and stuck the gun in the back of my waistband, like they do in cheap B flicks. Things were getting very real. I reined in my panic and walked as calmly as I could to the front door. I put my hands behind my head as if I was being held at gunpoint. I walked towards the driveway where there was a second man standing beside Steve's truck. Nancy was sitting on the back seat of the truck, her hands behind her back. The man was wrapping her ankles with duct tape. I was watching him like a hawk—every move he made. Even so, I noticed the hand gun lying on the truck's canopy.

Nancy couldn't see me but somehow the man sensed my approach and turned.

"Where's Frank?"

Still watching him, I half-turned and indicated by jerking my head that his partner was right behind me. He wasn't fooled—he didn't even move his eyes to look. They were focused on mine. As I locked eyes with him I could tell his decision had been made, even before he went for his gun. I pulled the .45 from my belt and shot him from less than three feet away. He dropped like a stone. I felt like doing the same. Instead I turned to help my wife. Nance had tape over her mouth; her hands and feet were bound. Otherwise she looked intact, though deathly pale and more than a little upset.

I freed her and retrieved the second gun.

"What's going on?"

"Oh my God! I have no idea! I had no choice, really. Had to do it. Hit him, I mean. The first guy. He was clearly a threat. I heard you shout. I didn't have time to think, really. I just hit him. I killed him. I *must* have killed him. I used a putter."

"What are you talking about? What the hell's going on?"

I took a deep breath. Surveyed the scene. Gathered what wits I could. And then I quickly explained what I thought had happened. Nance stared at me.

"Charlie, you saved us. They were going to take us in. He said they were bounty hunters. He kept calling me an illegal. I told him I was a Canadian. I said we were tourists. He said he didn't care and there's a bounty on us and to shut up. Then he taped my hands and feet. I was freaking out."

I looked around. I expected the gunshot, the one that was still ringing in my ears, would have brought people out of their homes but there was no one on the street. Nothing was moving. No one was looking. Maybe they were all at work. Maybe they didn't want to get involved. At any rate the gated community was quiet.

It had been a typical calm, hot, midweek afternoon in San Tan Valley, Arizona, land of the free, home of the brave. But now we had two dead guys on our hands. Seems the free and the brave wanted to capture seniors and collect some kind of bounty. Fortunately for us, their plan hadn't worked out.

"Nance, we have to get the body out of sight. Help me drag this guy behind the truck."

"Don't touch him. Leave it to the police. We should call them. It's a home invasion. What are you thinking?"

"I'm thinking he called you an illegal . . . they had guns . . . they thought they could turn us in for a bounty and they just may have been right. And if they *were* acting legally it wasn't a home invasion killing in self defense. It becomes murder. So no cops. Not yet, anyway. Now help me move him. We need to buy some time to figure out what's going on."

I had the guy's shoulders and lifted. Nancy, who is pretty strong for a sixty-six year old, grabbed his feet. We pulled him around to the back of the truck. The body was mostly hidden.

"Go inside the house and open the garage." Nance did as I asked and the garage door lifted. We heaved the body inside and closed the door.

"Charlie, there's a really big dead guy with a putter stuck in his temple in the hallway."

"I know. It was a small putter. He had a big head. I got lucky."

It just so happens that the San Tan Valley has immense wheeled trash and recycling barrels in its residential neighborhoods. As we pulled the body into the garage and noticed them we realized they were plenty big enough for a body and that instantly became our plan. Before we dumped the guy I went through his pockets.

"What are you looking for?"

"Well, there's the slim possibility that he was authorized in some way to take us in. Sounds kinda police-like. I want to see if he has any ID or papers."

I found his driver's license. His name was Peter something—I don't remember. There were a few dollars in his wallet. Various credit cards. Visa. Costco. I left them. He had a six inch folding knife that I pocketed and a small pouch of a dozen or so bullets, plus a full clip in his back pocket. I took those too. He was clad in denim and had one of those turquoise and silver belt buckles so favored in the southwest. Funny what sticks in your mind.

The first guy was bigger than I remembered from our brief encounter. It's hard to judge the size of someone lying in a heap on the floor but he was close to three hundred pounds, not all of it muscle. He wore huge baggy shorts, the kind with the line down the side. He had on a loose fitting sleeveless shirt exposing tattooed arms. The putter didn't improve his looks any but, to be fair, it didn't make them much worse, either. His face was scarred and pock-mocked and his beard and mustache were unfettered. He was an ugly, scary guy. I was very, very lucky to not have had a real altercation with him. Blessed be the putter.

Nancy and I rolled him onto a blanket so we could drag him the short distance to the garage. I checked his pockets but they were empty. We tipped a barrel on its side, pushed him in and levered it back up. We put him in the trash and got the other guy in recycling.

"You okay, sweetie?"

"Not really. I just killed two guys. I think I'm going to be sick. I can't stop shaking. It's kind of a jolt. Plus, now I'm terrified of getting caught by the cops."

"I'm just glad they didn't get us. I'm feeling relief, mostly. I was in the truck all taped up. I was completely helpless. I'll never forget that. At least you fought back and thank God you did. I can't believe you did that."

"I can't either. All instinct . . . primal."

"Sweetie?"

"What?"

"You have to calm down, although I'm not sure if *I* can. You did what you had to do. Even if we get caught, it was self defense. We may get in a lot of trouble over all this, but we can get through it if we don't panic."

"I hope so, Nance. I really do."

"So, now what?"

"Now we act like criminals cleaning up a crime scene. We clean up the kitchen, checking for blood. It's a tile floor so we can scrub it well. But look around the walls at head height, too. I hit the guy when he was standing. Look carefully everywhere. I'll go out with some cleaner and make sure the truck doesn't have blood on it. We'll throw the rags and the blanket in the washer when we're done. I sure hope there isn't any blood on the driveway. That'd be hard to remove and you know what a neat freak Steve is."

CHAPTER TWO — *Charlie*

For most of the few weeks we'd been enjoying Steve's vacation home in Arizona we hadn't watched television. Using our Netflix account from home we'd watched a few movies but we hadn't kept up with the news. Still, I seemed to recall something about Immigration and Customs Enforcement, commonly known as ICE, being instructed by the US administration to crack down on illegal immigrants and to stop sanctuary cities from helping undocumented people.

As I thought more about it, I remembered that we'd also become aware of some very subtle changes in Steve's neighborhood. When we first arrived there were a lot of Hispanic workers on the construction sites of new homes nearby. When we walked around those areas we made friendly overtures and said hola when it seemed appropriate. Initially we got a friendly greeting in return. But in the past week or so the response was more of silence and suspicion. No one said anything back. They just turned and walked away.

During the last few days, I now realized, we had seen fewer workers on the construction sites and fewer Latinos in the shopping areas we frequented. And the mood was different. As we only went out for dinner and groceries now and then it was hard to describe, but the vibes were off. Something was in the air.

Luis was Steve's gardener. He worked with his daughter, Sofía, and they dropped by every three days to spend half an hour sweeping leaves and generally tidying up. I'd met Luis very briefly the day we'd arrived. We'd chatted and cracked some jokes. I'd offered him and Sofía a cool drink and use of the bathroom. They declined, but politely. They were pleasant but a little wary. After that they came by as regular as clockwork.

But they hadn't been on the job today when we'd been expecting them. I noticed that, but didn't think much of it at the time. Now it was all starting to gel.

"I think the Immigration service is doing a crackdown. I don't know why but I can feel it. I think we'd better watch the news right now."

"But, even if they are, why us? We're not Mexicans. We're not illegals—we're snow-birds. Why would anyone want to kidnap us at gunpoint?"

"I don't know. That's why we have to watch the news."

An hour later it had become all too clear. A presidential order had been signed and a new program of enforcement was being implemented. We were classified as illegal aliens because we hadn't registered with the local police by the announced deadline. Apparently everyone who wasn't a US citizen had to register or a warrant was issued for their arrest. The deadline was yesterday. Someone had turned us in.

"That's insane," Nancy said. "We've only been here two weeks. We went through Immigration when we entered the country. Why would they need another check?"

"The warning that this was in the works has been out for a few months, it seems, but I guess it wasn't given much air time in Canada. Of course, we don't listen to the news that much at home either. It may not have been intended for Canadians but apparently the order was poorly worded. Plus, it seems that the greater Phoenix area, including the San Tan Valley, is the first area where the new enforcement is being implemented. They're emphasizing zero tolerance so that must mean tourists, too. It was a surprise. It was supposed to be. It was news to a lot of people, not just us."

"But those bounty hunters were ready."

Only Bambi and Garth from across the street knew we were here. They had a deal of sorts with Steve to watch his house. We'd met them when we arrived but we weren't overly impressed. Bambi was surly and impatient and seemed constantly irritated. Garth was obsequious. They appeared financially strained and obviously weren't happy as a couple. After our initial introduction we went our separate ways. My guess was they had turned us in to get a cut of the bounty.

"Bambi and Garth must have called those guys. Which means they knew they were coming. They may have seen what happened."

"Garth's normally at work during the day. Bambi's car isn't out front. She might be out with the kids. She probably missed the whole thing."

"Let's hope so. I guess if she had witnessed it, a bunch of cops would've been here by now."

"Well, at any rate, I don't think we should stay."

"Me neither. So, where do we go? With zero tolerance, going to the airport and trying to get our tickets changed would be stupid. Maybe we phone the Canadian Embassy and see what they have to say."

An hour on hold ended that plan.

"Charlie, let's phone Ben back home. Ask him to get through to the Embassy there and call us back."

"I have a feeling he's just going to be put on hold as well and I don't think we have time to wait. We need to leave as soon as possible. But at least text him and Katie to let them know what's up."

"Okay, and sweetie, I think we should head to the Canadian border."

"Well, three days of driving gets us to the border. Three days of sitting here gets us arrested. I agree"

"If Phoenix is the test city for all this, maybe if we go home via California things will lighten up a bit. We'll have to take Steve's truck but I'm sure he'll understand."

"Okay, Nance, let's get packed up and finalize our route once we're out of here."

A few minutes into our packing there was a rap at the door. We both froze. The rap was repeated. It wasn't a heavy knock; it was rapid and light. I had to answer it. The truck was out front. It was obvious we were inside. In my best imitation of a guy on the lam, I held the .45 in my right hand behind my back and firmly placed my left foot six inches behind the front door. I opened it a crack. It was Luis. He looked frightened.

"Luis. Come in."

Luis slipped inside. I subtly tucked the gun under my shirt and closed the door.

"Señor y señora, you must leave. It is dangerous here for you."

"I know. We just found out. Seems there's an immigration crackdown and it includes us."

"Señor, the danger is not just from Immigration. It is from the vigilantes also. They get a bounty if they bring you in. Most Latinos are not illegals, but no one is taking any chances. It is ICE *and* the vigilantes we are afraid of. They are everywhere."

"But you are safe, right? Sofía, too?"

"No, señor. No Latino is safe. It is dangerous for us all. I have a green card, señor, but I did not register again as I should have. Sofía is a Dreamer. She came with her mom almost twenty years ago when she was six. No papers, nothing. She was safe before because she came as a little child but, now that DACA is no more, she is an illegal. My grandson is a citizen but he is not safe either. He is just a baby and has to stay with Sofía. We all have to get out."

"But, if *you* had status, why didn't you register?"

"I have some misdemeanors from when I was young. That is enough, now, for them to deport me. Even with a green card. Nobody trusts Immigration right now, señor. Papers or no papers. ICE can do anything they want. They would send me to Eloy and I won't go back there. If they take me what is going to happen to Sofía and the baby? I could not take the chance."

"What's Eloy? Nancy asked.

"It is a big detention center for ICE. It is only forty minutes away from here, on the way to Tucson. It is a very bad place. Some guys are in for three months before they see a judge. And even then, what is the judge going to say, you are free to go? No way. You are given a public lawyer who goes to find your papers. The problem is the lawyers do not rush. Or maybe they are too busy. Even when you are released, it might take a week or more for the door to open."

"Sounds pretty bad, Luis. What was it like?" I asked.

"I was there twice. For no reason. Both times it took two weeks for them to figure out I have a green card. The second time I got beat up pretty bad. People get hurt, like I did. Sometimes they die there, señor. And Eloy is better than Florence. Florence is up the road and when Eloy is filled up, they send you there. That is a real supermax prison and there are some very scary dudes there. ICE is something you never want in your life, amigo. Today we leave Arizona and maybe sometime we come back. Maybe not."

"Thank you for coming to tell us about the danger, Luis. I understand your concern, more than you know. Are you safe to get home?"

"No señor. I came *here* to be safe. A group of vigilantes is in the community right now. I saw them. I believed this to be the best thing to do."

"Well, Luis, we're leaving. Come with us. You know the area. You can help us get out of here."

"Señor, you have license plates from Canada on your truck. The vigilantes will see you. They will stop you."

"Right. I think I know where I can steal some Arizona plates. You guys wait here—I'll let you know when the truck's ready to go."

I had noticed a car in the driveway of a house a few doors down which had not been driven in some time. It looked like the owner hadn't been living there for a while, either. I took the plates and threw Steve's plates into the back of the truck. I was back at the house in less than ten minutes.

It had struck me while I was out on the street that the next day was trash pickup. Some homes already had barrels out front, including Bambi and Garth's. I just didn't think it was right to leave my friend Steve trying to explain away the two dead bodies in his trash. I wheeled our heavy barrels out front of Bambi and Garth's and brought theirs to the curb by Steve's place. It might not stop the law, but it might slow it down, and if Bambi and Garth were inconvenienced in the process, so be it.

CHAPTER THREE

"Ben, Nancy texted me. I'm really concerned."

"Why didn't she text *me*? I'm her son."

"She knows I'm better at responding to messages. She said she and your dad are on the run from the police. They need us to help. She said there's a blanket warrant for the arrest of anyone who didn't register with US Immigration by a certain date and they hadn't."

"What? I didn't know that."

"Me neither. Obviously *they* didn't. Anyway, she seemed pretty worried. They're making a run for the border in Steve's truck. They want us to get information from the government to see what they should do. They already tried phoning the Canadian consulate down there but they couldn't get through. Seems like a lot of Canadians are in the same predicament and all hell is breaking loose."

"Screw that. I know my parents, Katie. I'm not doing their dirty work for them. Let *them* call the government. They're always pulling crazy stunts running around in foreign countries."

"Your mom sounded awfully serious. She said something that I think was intended to make you take notice."

"What?"

"She said they were armed and were very relieved to be. She said they needed the guns because they were frightened and in danger."

"Are you *kidding* me?"

"No, seriously."

"Really? That's crazy. How'd they get hold of guns? That has to be illegal. That's really nuts. I'm going to call them."

"She said they were likely going to be out of cell range for a while."

Ben took the phone and read the message. He sat there for a second. "I'll call someone in government to see what's really going on. It sounds pretty intense. Why don't you try my mom's friend, Jorgina, at Immigrant Services? She might have some information. And I'd better check with my sister to see if she's heard from them."

CHAPTER FOUR — *Charlie*

"What's the safest way out of the complex, Luis?"

"With your new plates you can drive past the vigilantes' trucks parked by the gate, señor. Just be an American. Do not act like a Canadian. I will hide in the back seat. You know how to get to Ocotillo Road, correct? Turn left and stay on it. Follow it for four miles. After we cross the aqueduct, turn left at the next road—no name. I can get out of the back then and direct you."

We passed the trucks gathered at the gate and got down to Ocotillo without incident. Luis took us off the pavement and down the unmarked road to another track as we drove deeper into the desert past small shanties and clusters of trailers and old recreational vehicles. Luis and Sofía looked clean and presentable when they were tending gardens, but they lived in an impermanent, and what looked like an empty, itinerant community.

"Where is everyone, Luis?"

"Some, perhaps, are hiding, señor. Steve's truck is frightening for them. No one out here drives a shiny new truck like this. But many have left already. They went when they heard what was happening. That is our casita over there, señor."

We stopped in front of an old broken-down fifth wheel with four flat tires. A rusty Nissan pickup truck made it a matching all-flat-tired ensemble. The place looked deserted. As soon as Luis climbed out, Sofía burst from the front door, a toddler on her hip, and the three held each other tight.

After Luis explained what was happening Sofía insisted on giving Nance and me explicit instructions for the route out of town that was most likely to succeed. She offered to take us. We refused. Her instructions would have to be sufficient.

"Where are *you* going, Sofía? When are you leaving?"

Sofía looked at Luis and they spoke to each other in Spanish for a minute.

"We are leaving now, señor," said Luis. "We were waiting for another, but he has been detained. At least we know he was taken to the police station. He has a green card so they will release him later, I think. Maybe he is safer in jail. I think he will be okay. But we have to leave now. This place is known to a lot of people. It is just a matter of time before vigilantes come."

"That truck isn't taking you far."

"We will walk, señor. Across the desert to Mexico. It is safer for us in the desert."

"That's crazy. You need water. You need protection. It's almost a hundred and fifty miles to the border. And once you cross over you're in Sonora. The cartels rule that state. We're in danger but attempting that is even more dangerous. You guys better come with us."

"It is not safe for you, señor."

"It's safer for us if we have a guide. It's safer for you if you have transportation. I think you should come with us to get where you want to go. Then we'll head north. We were thinking California is the best place to head for, anyway. At least they're not implementing the crackdown there yet. What do you think?"

"California is best, but not arriving from the south. Most people running from Arizona will choose California. The farther north we go, the fewer vigilantes, I think. It is only six hours to Los Angeles on I-10. I suspect many will go that way."

"Fair enough. Maybe we should head up to Flagstaff and then head west. It'll be a few extra hours of driving but hopefully it'll be safer."

Luis and his daughter gathered some belongings and bottled water and piled in with Sofía's toddler. She introduced him as León and, us to him, as Abuelo Charlie and Abuela Nancy. He gave us a shy smile and then turned to bury his head in his mom's shoulder.

As we were pulling out of the shanty compound another truck was coming in.

"Vigilantes!" hissed Luis. "Don't stop."

"Trust me on this, Luis. Just look frightened."

"Easy peasy, gringo." he said. Normally that would've made me laugh.

The dirt road was narrow. Two vehicles could pass by each other only with some cooperation. The big Ford pickup coming at us seemed a little reluctant to proceed at first, but neither was the driver conceding us passing room. I pulled the gun out from under my shirt and draped my left arm out the window casually showing the .45. The truck pulled over to let us pass. As we crawled by, the driver asked, through his open window, "Any luck?"

I gestured towards the family in the backseat, "Got me three. The rest lit out for the hills. Three's enough for me. Good huntin' to ya."

That worked. The Ford kept going and so did we. I slipped the gun back into the car. Luis still hadn't seen it. I left it that way.

"Grandes cajones, señor. Gracias."

CHAPTER FIVE — *Charlie*

As she turned to look at him from the front seat Nancy asked Luis, "Do you have family in California?"

"No!" Luis's answer was uncharacteristically abrupt. Nancy turned away but I noticed Sofía looking imploringly at her father.

"My no-good, criminal son-in-law lives in Los Angeles. He is a drug dealer. An ex-con. Cops hate him. I hate him. Maybe Jesus loves him but I do not think so. He is a bad hombre."

"Papa." Sofía said, and then seemingly stopped herself from speaking further.

Luis turned away and looked out the window. This obviously wasn't a conversation he wanted to be having.

Nancy looked at Sofía. I knew there was more to be heard on this topic but this wasn't the time. The two women shared a brief glance and Nancy changed the subject, "Aren't you going to fill up, Charlie?"

* * * * *

Patrolman Terry O'Reilly wheeled the cruiser into the gas station and got out. He went into the store, bought a can of coke, and got back in just as a gray Avalanche pulled up to the gas bar. Looked legit. Still, way too many trucks full of idiots looking for bounties right now. If they *were* legit, they shouldn't be out here. They should be home and locked down. This was a bad day to be out on the streets of San Tan Valley.

He looked to see who got out of the truck. The tinted windows made it hard to see inside but he knew there was a woman in the front passenger seat. She was turned away from him, looking into the back seat, but he could tell she had white hair. Probably talking to her dog or her grandkids or something.

The driver looked ex-military. Crew cut. Stocky. Over sixty, that's for sure, but he moved okay. He was just going about his business getting gas. The scenario didn't fit any profile Terry was interested in. He turned the key and fired up the cruiser.

"Four four zero, this is zero six six. I'm at Ocotillo and North Ironwood. No traffic. Nothing. Heading out to the end of Ocotillo. Over."

"Roger that, zero six six. You goin' to the Mex camp there?"

"That's the plan."

"Be careful out there, Terry. There could be vigilantes."

Terry spun the wheel of the black Ford Victoria and headed south. Thinking of the people out at the camp, he now regretted taking the time to get a coke.

* * * * *

I gassed up and got back in the truck. After a few minutes of driving, I took a deep breath. "Luis, I killed two guys."

"Señor . . . ?"

"Back at the house. Kind of a home invasion thing. Before you got there. One guy grabbed Nance and took her outside. I came in from the backyard and hit the first guy with a golf club. It was instinctive. Then I picked up his gun and walked outside and shot the second guy. We put their bodies in the trash bins."

"Señor!"

"I know. Crazy. Freaks me out just thinking about it. It wasn't right not to tell you, though. I'm sorry. It seemed like it was mostly just a horrible accident. But now I know they were vigilantes and they knew we were there at the house. If *they* knew we were there, then others do, too. If you don't want to be associated with us I understand. We'll drop you off wherever you want."

"Señor, you a cop or something?"

"No, Luis, not a cop. Not a soldier. Just an old guy reacting in the moment. Scary, though. Hitting the first guy was just a reaction. Automatic. And I wasn't planning on shooting the second guy. But I picked up the gun. It just went off, really. I didn't know what I thought I was going to do with it and then . . . it just happened. The weird part is that I wasn't frightened, at least not then. It was like slow-mo, you know? But right now, I'm terrified. Can't stop shaking."

Luis looked down. Sofía looked at me. They were trying to make sense of this. So was I. "Sorry . . . I owed it to you to tell you."

"You had no choice. You acted in self defense." Nancy patted my hand. "I'm glad you did what you did, Charlie. They could have killed us. You can't blame yourself."

"I don't. Not really. I think it was the right thing to do and, anyway, they were in our house with guns and had taken you. Right or wrong, it was a natural reaction. The part I feel guilty about is that, without thinking, we've involved Luis and Sofía. So far, we've just been running. We're not being smart about this at all."

"Señor, if you had not helped us, the vigilantes in the pickup truck would have taken us in, or worse. Being with you saved us. We are grateful. But if the cops are looking for you, as well as the vigilantes, maybe we should leave you. Perhaps we are in more danger now being with you."

"Fair enough, Luis. Just tell me where you want to go. You know someone in the Phoenix area? What about up near Scottsdale? It's a better district. Likely fewer vigilantes, I'm thinking."

"Si. Mi amigo works at a resort there. He will take us in."

"Papa. We promised Charlie and Nancy we'd get them out of here safely. We can't leave them."

"But, Sofía . . ."

"We're staying with them. We're leaving Phoenix and I want to go to California. Be quiet, papa. No more talking."

We all rode in silence for a minute. Sofía had a powerful voice when she felt strongly and, oddly, that had a relaxing effect on me. I caught a small smile from Nance, too. Even Luis didn't argue further. It wasn't much of anything but I stopped trembling and concentrated on driving. Maybe it was because someone in the truck seemed to know what they were doing.

I was surprised Sofía had spoken up so forcefully. Prior to this she had seemed subdued, her face hidden by her hoodie. She wore no makeup or jewelry. I hadn't seen her smile, except at little León. You had to look twice but, if you did, she was a truly beautiful young woman. I wondered then if the life she was living was the one she'd imagined for herself.

Luis interrupted my thoughts. "Take the highway east, señor, but look ahead before you do. The vigilantes will probably set up near the exits. The next ramp is just a few miles up."

I couldn't see exactly what was causing it, but it looked like traffic was getting congested way up ahead. Luis noticed it, too. "Take that road at the hole in the fence, señor. It is on someone's land and it leads through the desert for a long while. We will find a way to join up to the highway later."

I pulled off the highway and onto the shoulder. When I had slowed sufficiently, I turned the truck down the dirt slope into the ruts that passed through what was obviously nothing more than a break in the fence.

Desert scrubland bordered all the major roads I had seen in the area and this was no exception. I had no idea what the surface would be like to drive on and checked the dash for the 4x4 option, just in case. It wasn't necessary. Not here, anyway. Here it was hard and flat. Ugly, small, dry bushes scraped against the truck as I weaved left and right to find the clearest path. After the first hundred feet or so the tracks faded out and desert terrain was the only option. I drove at less than five miles an hour. After a while Luis suggested heading north to see if we could intersect with the highway. More than once I had to resume an easterly direction as we encountered various obstacles of scrub and old fencing that prevented me from driving parallel to the highway.

After an hour or so we could see the highway again. It was a discouraging sight. Elevated at least fifteen feet from the desert floor, it was built on a bed of rocks and gravel. I couldn't gain access much of the time because of the ubiquitous fence running alongside it. If I found an opening and had a bit of a run at it, though, I was pretty sure I could climb up the slope to the road. The only other problem was that I was inviting a collision if I came up too fast and ended up across a lane of traffic in the middle of the interstate.

"Not to worry, señor. There are breaks in the fence all over. And they are always where the slope and access is good. These breaks are used by locals for hunting and by Mexicans migrating north. Often coyotes use them for smuggling people. Just keep driving until we find a good one."

Luis was right. Minutes later I spied a hole in the fence leading to a less severe incline that allowed access to the highway. I stopped the vehicle, got out and walked the route. It was easily navigated, requiring only the removal of a few rocks to make it passable. I asked Luis to climb to the road and give me a signal when it was clear enough to make the attempt.

A Chevy Avalanche is a luxury, four-door crew cab pickup truck. This fairly new model was top end and in great shape. It was equipped with a powerful V-8 and four wheel drive with a high and a low option. I chose the higher gear because I wanted to hit the gravel slope with some speed without the engine revving too high. In this situation I figured momentum was as important as power. The fifteen foot high slope was maybe only fifty feet or so long and I guessed at a twenty-five degree slope of loose gravel. This was not a time to be hesitant.

I intended to hit it at a bit of an angle so as to transfer some weight to the front wheels as the truck climbed. A real worry was the tires. They were big and new, mounted on twenty inch rims, all of which suggested grip, but they were highway tires and it would have been better to be sporting all-terrain tread. I intended suggesting that to Steve the next time I saw him.

When Luis signaled I accelerated and I hit the slope at between fifteen and twenty miles per hour. The big truck leaned because of the angle of attack and was half way up before I felt the tires trying to find traction. I kept the speed relatively constant at first but then had to back off the accelerator slightly to accommodate the effects of gravity overcoming the initial momentum. The last ten feet saw a bit of spraying gravel but we crested the climb at walking speed. It was as if I did it every day.

"Good one, señor. I didn't think you had a chance."

"Luis, what are you saying? You said coyotes and local hunters use these fence breaks all the time."

"Si, señor. But they climb up and down to their vehicles. They don't drive."

CHAPTER SIX

Terry pulled his cruiser into the dusty compound and got out. It looked deserted. He recognized the old Ford pickup with the Confederate flag bumper-sticker parked in front of Luis' place. That was where his attention was focused when he heard someone behind him.

"Ain't illegal, officer. I got my rights. Government put a bounty on illegals and I got as much right as anyone to collect. You got no reason to interfere."

Terry looked at Early Mack and knew that his brother Lyle couldn't be too far away. He glanced around and couldn't see Lyle, but that probably just confirmed he was there somewhere.

"Got no problem, Early. Just came out to warn Luis to be careful of shitheads like you, that's all. You know Luis and Sofía are legal, right? You can't take them in."

"Can if they haven't registered. And we won't know if they registered or not 'til we take 'em in. Take in that snot-nosed kid, too. It's authorized."

Terry cursed the Federal government for the umpteenth time that day. This crackdown had not been thought through. Perfectly legitimate people were going to be forcibly arrested by untrained imbeciles for no other reason than suspicion laced with bigotry. There was no freedom in Phoenix that day and it was starting to feel like there was never going to be freedom anywhere in the country again.

"Well then, Early, you go about your business, but let me make something perfectly clear. You hurt someone, anyone, illegal or not, and I'll take you in. You may get off because you're a lying son of a bitch, but I'll arrest you and charge you for something every time I see your ass. You got that? You do this goddamn job right or, so help me God, I'll make your life even worse than it already is. You got that, asshole?

"Loud and clear, officer. Me and Lyle gonna treat these spics like family, we will. Real nice. Hell, I may even kiss Sofía a few times. She's a nice piece of ass."

Terry knew he was being baited. He just ignored it and looked around. He couldn't help but ponder how Early and Lyle normally treated family.

"Luis! Sofía! You guys here? C'mon out if you want. They can't take you if I'm here. This is a good time to get safe. C'mon out."

"I think that Avalanche got the last of 'em, the bastard. Said he had three. Wished me good huntin' and knew all the time there wasn't no one here. Wasted my time."

"What Avalanche?"

"Silver-gray. Old motherfucker was armed—held his piece out the window as we passed on the road. He was all casual-like. Said he had three in the back. Couldn't see 'cause of the windows were dark. But I believed him."

Terry spun around and went back to his car. As he got in, he saw Lyle appear from the shadows. Lyle was carrying—looked like a pump-action. Five minutes later, Terry was on the highway heading back toward the gas station.

"Four four zero, this is zero six six. The trailers were empty. Luis was gone. I'm guessing Sofía and the kid are with him. They may have been picked up by a vigilante. Early and Lyle Mack were there at the trailers, snooping around, and said as much. Think I saw the truck earlier and the guy driving it. Fits the description Early gave of a truck driving out of Luis' place. Could be vigilantes. Could be friends. Could be anybody. Would you check with ICE to see if Luis or Sofía has been brought in?"

"I'll try, Terry, but they're run off their feet right now. I doubt they've even identified and booked everyone who's been brought in already. I'll get back to you if I find out anything."

Terry thought about stopping at the gas station and checking the security tapes, but to what end? Plus, it would take forever. Guy buys gas. Guy leaves. Maybe getting the plates would help but he decided not to stop—too much else going on. A few miles up the road was an entrance to the freeway and the goddamn vigilantes were setting up a roadblock there. Someone was going to have an accident. He'd get up there, get rid of them, and maybe come back to check out the plates. This whole thing was getting out of hand.

* * * * *

Aba paced the front room. "Where the fuck are they? Why isn't Sofía calling me?"

"Relax, man. Luis knows what he's doing. He'll get 'em out. The real question is will she come to you? I don't think so. You two are done."

"Fuck you, Miguel! Who the fuck else can take care of her, man? I got her off drugs, man. *And* I'm the fucking father. They *got* to come to me."

"They hate you, man. Face it. Luis thinks you hooked her up and she thinks you just cut her off. You lost her, bro. You went to jail. I'm the one who kept her straight, not you, bro. Do the crime, do the time, lose your familia. That's the way that shit goes down. She left your ass, man, and she ain't comin' back. You got unrequited love, man."

"What you sayin'? What the fuck is unquiet love, man? You talkin' shit."

"Unrequited, dawg. It means you love her, she don' love you. Simple, man."

"Fuck you and that quiet love shit, man. I'm gonna find her and save my baby boy. Fuck man, I may even save that motherfucker, Luis. He gets 'em out and all is forgiven, dude."

"You crazy motherfucker, it's them who forgives. Not you. You fucked up, man."

* * * * *

"Ben, I got through to Jorgina at Immigrant Services. She said it's bad down there and your parents could be in real trouble. Her office phones are ringing off the hook. Canadians in the US are freaked. Most of them didn't know about any registry or crackdown. And a lot of them are being hauled in by vigilantes. She said your parents should get to the nearest Canadian consulate and get escorted to the airport."

"Yeah, my sister said much the same thing. I couldn't reach anyone in government—they have a friggin' phone tree that never ends."

"Well, Jorgina said some of the stories she's hearing are pretty ugly. Lots of people are afraid. Phoenix is a test city and tourists are being included in the sweep. The news says it's unclear if they're supposed to be, but the vigilantes don't care. If they bring in a non-American, they think they get the bounty."

"Who are the vigilantes? Has the US privatized enforcement of immigration laws or something?"

"The immigration enforcement people figured they didn't have enough officers to do a state wide sweep of Arizona so they're using freelance contracted bounty hunters. Apparently regulations exist, but they aren't really enforced, so every red-neck gun-toting Wyatt Earp wannabe thinks he's authorized to go out and bring people in."

"And what the hell is this bounty crap?"

"All I know is it's two hundred dollars a head for any non-American who hasn't registered. If you're on a watch list or have a warrant, or anything in addition to just not registering, that bounty is doubled."

"Well that's good news, actually. Two old, white Canadians would be hard to spot as illegals and, even if they were picked up, they're less likely to be worth double. If I was a vigilante, I'd be looking for Muslims and Mexicans. That's where the money is."

"Great! I married a natural-born bounty hunter. Would you go for the Asians, too, Ben?"

"Look. I'm just saying that my parents are not high profile. They're in danger, but not as much danger as a Muslim or a Mexican. I mean if I was a vigilante . . ."

"Never mind, I really don't want to know how you're thinking. I checked with the nearest Canadian consulate in Phoenix. Took forever to get through. They'll help your parents get to the airport. They'll have to pay for another flight and they'll be held for at least forty-eight hours prior to leaving to make sure they aren't wanted or on some list. Jorgina said there've been some horror stories so far. Lots of people missing. They get escorted to Immigration, the Canadian Consulate staff leaves, and nothing more is heard. I sure as hell wouldn't report in."

"Katie, this sounds bizarre. And Canada is cooperating with this?"

"I think Ottawa is going to protest, or lodge a formal complaint or something, but what are they going to do? There are thousands of Canadian citizens down there with only a few dozen embassy and consulate staff to deal with them. Canadians overseas have never been that well protected by our government and that isn't changing right now."

"I wish we could get them on the phone . . ."

"I know, but I've texted them the information I found out. I asked them to call. But I have no idea how we can really help them."

CHAPTER SEVEN — *Charlie*

We were heading east on the Superstition Freeway. Luis said the route through Apache Junction was likely the safest. It was possibly a little dangerous around the main intersection because of all the roads meeting there but, after that, we'd be heading out to Scottsdale. We covered the distance to the Idaho off-ramp and it looked good. I caught the light and turned left. We only had to get through a couple more miles to reach the junction, turn left there and we'd almost be in the clear.

I didn't even see the police cruiser sitting off to the side of the road.

* * * * *

Terry watched the gray Avalanche go by. He couldn't see who was inside. They weren't speeding. Still, seeing it again was enough for him. Something was trying to get his attention and he had a very strong hunch what it was. He headed out and followed for a bit. He ran the plates. They belonged to a Volkswagen back in San Tan Valley. That old guy had bad plates when he pulled in for gas. Probably had Luis, Sofía and León on board, as well. He didn't even hesitate to pull in when I was parked there, Terry thought. But he's not heading in the direction of the ICE locations. What's he up to?

He called it in. "Four four zero, this is zero six six. I have a late model Chevy Avalanche traveling north on Idaho. Matches the description of the suspect vehicle back at the camp that I reported earlier. It has fictitious plates. They belong to a Volkswagen in San Tan Valley. Any reports of a stolen Chevy Avalanche?"

"No, Terry, nothing. But we did have a call from a neighbor who says they think they heard shots fired on Empress Tree Lane. You wanna head over and check it out?"

"No, not right now. First I'm going to pull this guy over and see what's up. Get me the information on the shots fired and leave it with me. I'll get to it later."

"Roger that."

* * * * *

Sofía was half asleep. León was snoring, a whispery cute little wheeze. Luis looked alert. Nance was trying to get service on the phone. I was watching the navigation screen and trying to be invisible. I failed.

The siren just went whoop whoop. The lights flashed. That was it. I pulled over. This could be bad.

"Luis, get Sofía and León on the floor. Cover them up. Duck down. They may be looking for Mexicans. Be still."

The cruiser just sat there for a long minute. The cop was in the car sizing me up. But why? I wasn't speeding. Oh no! Of course, the plates were showing up on the cop's computer as belonging to another vehicle. Damn.

"Nance, this looks like trouble. Think we should run?"

"No. Don't be stupid. There are a gazillion cops and now a bunch of vigilantes. We can't run. Just try to cooperate and talk your way through it."

That didn't go down well with me. I hate cooperating at the best of times. I really hate cooperating with the authorities. I have a bit of a problem in that regard. But I couldn't see much of a choice.

"Afternoon, sir. Can I see your license and registration."

I handed him my Canadian license and Steve's registration.

"Not your car, sir?"

I immediately saw my way out of this. 'Not my car' was going to be my explanation.

"No, Officer. It belongs to my friend Steve. He has a house down here. We're borrowing it for a few weeks. Just vacationing."

"I notice your friend's house is on Empress Tree Lane. Just had a call about shots fired there. You know anything about that?"

"No, sir. Been out most of the day. Pretty quiet neighborhood, though."

"Yeah, I know. Where you been today?"

At this point my anti-authoritarian feelings started to rise. It seemed like a good place to try and put an end to this line of questioning.

"Officer, I know I wasn't speeding. Did I do something wrong?"

Terry stepped back and unclipped his holster. He put his hand on his gun and said very calmly, "Sir, please step out of the vehicle. Keep your hands where I can see them. Now."

I looked at him. He looked serious. He looked competent. He looked like he knew something but I didn't know what it could be, except for the plates, and I was going to play ignorant on that. I got out of the car. Kept my hands behind my head. He grabbed one arm, spun me around and slammed me against the side of the truck. I felt the first hand-cuff click into place and then the second one.

"Terry, is that you? It's me, Luis. I have Sofía here, and the baby."

The officer immediately stepped back and shouted at me, "Get down! Get down on the ground, now."

I knew he was pointing his gun at me but I really didn't want to get down on the ground. One of my knees doesn't bend very well. Still, he seemed upset, and it seems that cops tend to shoot people here, so I started to slowly get down on my good knee. I was going to try to get down on one knee and then explain the problem. I half expected to be kicked forward on my face. This was getting to be more than just a little annoying.

"Terry! Terry, no! El es mi amigo. He saved us. Terry, he saved us from the vigilantes."

The officer didn't kick me to the ground but he was not ready to give up the option. He held the gun pointed at me and looked at Luis.

"C'mon, Luis. Talk to me. Quickly. I don't like this guy. The truck has bad plates. He's up to something. Did he kidnap you? You can tell me now. Tell me, Luis. Where's Sofía?"

"Terry! *I* stole the plates. I had to. His truck had plates from Canada. There were vigilantes around. We had to look like a local truck. I took the plates. We have the old ones in the back. Terry, this is a good guy. Please let him up."

Terry risked a look inside. He saw Sofía holding León close. He was whimpering just a little. She had tears in her eyes. She said softly, "Terry, we're okay. These are our friends."

Terry holstered his service revolver and, still being careful, helped me up. He pushed me against the truck again, but more gently than the first time. He removed the cuffs and told me to stay where I was. I watched him put his cuffs away as he surveyed the scene.

"Luis, please get out of the truck and stand over there by the front of my car." He gestured at Nancy, "Ma'am, please get out of the truck and stand in front of it. I'll be right with you. No talking, please."

Nance got out and stood at the front. I stood at the side as instructed and this Terry guy walked back towards Luis. They exchanged a few words and the cop seemed to relax some. Then he walked over to the passenger side of the truck and opened the door to talk to Sofía. That lasted only seconds.

Then he came back to my side and said, "You have stolen plates. I could take you in for that. Luis tells me you got him and Sofía out of their place just in time. He didn't mention that you had a gun. Neither did Sofía. You have a gun, don't you?"

"Yes."

"A permit to carry?"

"No. It's not even my gun. It's stolen."

Terry looked at me hard. I said, "Long story. But, let's just say, a sloppy vigilante wasn't paying attention and I was."

He stepped away and a few steps later he was speaking to Nancy. That conversation was the longest. I didn't realize that he was corroborating everyone's statements with her. I found it unnerving. Finally Terry took Nancy by the arm and politely walked her towards me. Then he directed me to walk over to Luis. The four of us were gathered at the front of his cruiser.

"Seems you are the proverbial good guy doing everything wrong, mister. Your Canadian plates may be a signal to the vigilantes, but the stolen plates are a big fucking target to the police or ICE personnel. All they have to do is run these plates and they'll assume the truck is stolen. You'd be better off with the Canadian plates. And, since Luis confessed to stealing them, which I don't believe for a second, I'm going to let you off. You're lucky they haven't been reported missing yet. Get those stolen plates off your truck and your own plates back on. I'm taking the Arizona plates to return before any more damage is done. I have to go to Empress Tree next, anyway."

Before anyone could react, Nancy retrieved the Canadian plates, walked over to the front of the truck, pulled out her Swiss Army knife, made the exchange, and then did the same with the rear plates. Took only a couple of minutes. When she handed the plates to the officer, he was smiling, "Looks like you've done that before, ma'am."

"I have," she smiled back.

"Now you know I have to confiscate the gun. I know you think you need it and maybe you do. But I have to take it. I'm going to say I found it on Empress Tree somewhere. Fits with the report. Should be okay. And I think you guys should get out of the area as soon as possible. Luis says you think going north makes the most sense and I agree. But make no mistake, there are idiots with guns all over the place and, even though Phoenix is the centre for the ICE crackdown, technically it's state-wide. All the action so far seems to be centered around here though, so hopefully you'll be okay."

"We are going with them, Terry. We can help them and there is nothing for us right now in Arizona. I cannot take Sofía and León back to the trailer."

"Luis, don't be crazy. You and Sofía can come with me. I can get you a safe place to hide out. You can stay at my place if you want. The road is more dangerous than Phoenix, Luis. Think of your grandson."

"No, mi amigo. I am thinking of never coming back here. Lots of good people here, amigo, but too many bad ones right now. The government is going loco. I have no family but Sofía and León, so anywhere I go with them is home for me."

"Officer, as long as they're with us, we'll help them the best we can, gun or no gun." I walked over to the truck, felt under the seat, and pulled out one of the guns–the one I'd used to shoot the guy. I quickly wiped it with my shirt and then I held it at arm's length with my fingers pinched through the trigger guard to show that it was impossible to use. I needn't have bothered. Terry wasn't even looking in my direction.

When Terry eventually took the gun he said, "You said there was a long story as to how you got this?"

"Yeah, too long for right now. If you don't mind Officer, we really should get going. I'm already scared. So is everyone else and it's going to be dark soon. I'd really like to put some miles on this truck. Suffice to say, the gun isn't mine. It was on the ground. I just picked it up. Seriously."

"And brandished it towards some lowlifes to get Luis out."

"Yeah. And brandished it like I was a hard case. It worked."

Terry waved us off, but not without giving Sofía a hug and kissing the top of León's head. He obviously cared for them all. And then he headed back towards Empress Tree Lane where he would end up finding two dead bodies. I felt guilty lying by omission to a good man but it seemed like too much of a risk to tell him more right now.

"You have Terry's phone number, Luis?"

"I do. Why? You want to call him?"

"Yeah, when I get back to Canada I'll phone and tell him the truth about what happened. I think I have to."

"Maybe when you get back to Canada, señor, I will call him and tell him. Maybe you stay under the radar, okay?"

"Okay, Luis. Thanks. One condition, though. Stop calling me señor and call me Charlie. I think you can do that, can't you?"

"I was not calling you señor, señor. I was calling you senior. You are an old man."

"Katie messaged, Charlie. She said that the official advice is for us to get to the Canadian consulate in Phoenix. The staff there will escort us to Immigration at the airport. But no guarantees. We may get put on a plane but we may not. If we're on a list of any kind we'll be arrested. If that happens no one knows where we'd go or for how long. The way Katie's message read she was suggesting that we *not* go."

"Well, we're not on a list yet, but I think we have to go on the assumption that we may be by the time Terry is finished at Steve's house."

"I agree."

"If it ever comes to us getting apprehended by ICE we should assume they know nothing about the shooting and answer accordingly. I guess I'm saying don't admit to anything. Plead Miranda or something."

"You don't plead Miranda! They have to read you your Miranda rights. That's your right to remain silent, etcetera, although I know how hard *that* would be for you. But surely you've watched enough cop shows to know that."

"Whatever."

* * * * *

"Charles, maybe we shouldn't drive at night."

"What do you mean, Luis? You want to stop?"

"No. But in the daytime there is more traffic on the road. We blend in more. We can see better if we are being chased or there is a roadblock ahead. Sofía and León are going to need a little break from the backseat. I think we should seriously consider a new plan."

It was almost five o'clock. Traffic was still heavy. It was a hundred and forty-five miles to Flagstaff. It would get dark within the hour. Darker, anyway. I was thinking that most illegals might instinctively choose to travel by night. But daylight was better for us. We were somewhat camouflaged by Nance and me being white—we would be expected to be on the road in the daytime.

"You're right. We should get off the road. Let's find a hotel. The more upscale the better. The more expensive it is, the less likely there will be vigilantes around."

"What about us?"

"What do you mean?"

"Sofía and I look suspicious going into a fancy hotel."

"You may be right. Nancy and I'll check in. We'll pay for two adjoining rooms. The staff at the front desk will just assume we want separate rooms. We'll get in and let you guys in a side door. No sense waving a flag."

I took the entrance to Old West Highway and drove to the junction. The Best Western was on the left. It looked good enough.

"Stay low, Luis. They can't see into the truck. I'm going to see if I can get a couple of rooms at the end of the building. I can see exits there. If I can park near an exit, we can let you in and you'll be exposed for less time. Just remember, though, there'll be security cameras, so when you come to the door walk in like you own the place, okay?"

* * * * *

Things were going well. Pleasantries and smiles from the young woman at the front desk. Then she asked for identification and a credit card. "Sir, I notice you're Canadian."

"Yes."

"Sir, just for your information, all hotels in Arizona are obliged to notify ICE of any guests who cannot produce their registration stamp. Do you have your stamp, sir?"

I had no idea what she was talking about but it made sense for the powers that be to document registration and I was guessing that it came in the form of a permit or a stamp on our passports. "Oh, you mean the stamp on our passports?"

She was visibly relieved when I said that. "Yes sir, I have to see your passport. It's the law. It's not right, but there's nothing we can do. We can lose our license if I don't confirm it."

"Oh, okay. But all that crap is in our suitcases somewhere. I'm going to have to go get it. By the way, have you actually had to turn in anyone who wasn't registered with Immigration?"

"Not so far, sir. Most people just change their minds and leave. Since I haven't registered them as guests, there's no need to report anything."

"Where do they go?"

"No idea, sir. Every hotel in the state has to do this. If another hotel says they don't, they're lying and I guess they take your money and then collect the bounty when they report you. But, I don't know that for sure. That's just what they say."

"Who says?"

"We have a lot of foreign staff here, sir. The entire tourism industry is built on low wage workers and they tend to be foreign born. We have a lot of staff members from Mexico and the Philippines. And we tried to make sure everyone here registered when they were supposed to. But some disappeared around that time. We don't know if they just chose to leave or if they were swallowed up in the ICE sweep. We lost five staff. The ones remaining warned me about the other hotels."

"Well, then. Good to know. Thanks. I guess I'll just go out to the truck now. Get the passports . . ."

"Good luck, sir."

* * * * *

As I pulled out of the lot I explained what the woman had said and added, "Hotels are not an option."

"Charles, I am sure mi amigo will find a place for us. The resort where he works is not far. I can call him to arrange it."

Luis' friend said that he'd help. He also suggested taking the main roads as the police were clearing away roadblocks and, during the last of rush hour, it was the safest and fastest route. We went down Apache Trail to the 202, jumped on to it and headed west until we changed over to the 101. We didn't see any road blocks on the freeway but we did see a few clusters of jammed traffic on some of the side roads. They looked like checkpoints, just like you might see in some warring nation, complete with guys standing in pickup truck beds holding assault rifles. Arizona is an open carry state and people can carry guns all they like. And obviously they were liking it a lot.

Our instructions were to take the Pima exit off 101 and turn left on Princess. Then we were to follow the signs to the sports complex and we'd be met by Luis' friend, Bobby, at the entrance. The drive took about twenty-five minutes. Bobby was there.

Once he confirmed that Luis and Sofía were in the truck he jumped in beside Nancy. He directed us up North Hayden. He told me to turn in at the Desert Oasis Resort. It looked nice.

"Bobby, we can't stay here. They'll report us."

"They have to report you if you register, Charlie. You're not going to be registered guests. We're the cleaning staff. We're the maintenance staff and some of us are at the front desk. We're even part of management. The only place we're not in the majority is upper management and security. And we even have one or two Chicanos there."

"We can't rely on so many people to keep us a secret, Bobby. Bounty is bounty. Someone will turn us in."

"No one will know. I'm in maintenance. I can go anywhere. The safest place for you is in one of the expensive suites. I'll tell the front desk we have a plumbing problem. They'll take the room offline. I can't do it for two suites, you'll have to share, but I'll make sure it's nice."

We had a spacious two bedroom suite with a fold out couch. It was great. Bobby took some cash to bring us all pizza and beer and we enjoyed our luxurious surroundings. Hey, at least at that moment, being on the run wasn't all bad.

CHAPTER NINE

"Miguel, are you okay?"

"It's all good, Sofía, I can grab enough money for us. He knows I deserve it. Maybe I'll leave Aba a note. Shit, I hate buggin' out on him like this, but, fuck! I gotta get out of this shit. I gotta do this. I got a kid. I'm glad you're comin' back. I miss you. But, it's a bit too soon, baby. I haven't been able to tell Aba about us, ya know. It's not easy. I just ain't ready to get out yet."

"Tell him about us or don't. I don't care. What's to do? You already handle the cash and the inventory. Just grab some money and get out."

"Not that simple. The game's got rules. You don't rip off your boss for no good reason. I'd be a target. Plus it's about you and me. It's a man thing—I gotta tell 'im."

"How 'bout this? Aba is cooperating with the police. He's a snitch. He turned. He gonna give everyone up."

"Never gonna happen. Everyone knows Aba got no time for cops. He'd never turn. He already done time and didn't talk. No one gonna believe that shit."

"Then tell Aba I'm comin' back. But you tell him I'm travelin' with two gringos who killed two people in Arizona. He can trade that information for something. He'll do somethin' with it for sure."

"How that gonna help us?

"You'll see, Miguel. It'll make a little hell and keep him distracted. I'm bringing your son to you. You gotta man up, homie. Now's the time to get your share and get out. You have to. I can't stop this truck from getting there so we gotta make it work for us if we gonna be together. And, if we gonna be together, you know you have to leave, right? Aba would kill you if he knew León wasn't his. He'd go crazy, man. He might kill us both. And I ain't gonna be stuck with Aba, again. Never. It's you or no one for me, Miguel."

"You right. I'll do it. I want out, I really do. Just gotta think. Where are you?"

"We're in Scottsdale. Stayin' the night. Right now Luis and the gringos are talkin' about going to LA, but they wanna go to Flagstaff first. I can't make 'em do anything, but it's the best way to get away from the vigilantes and at least we're headed for California."

"Okay. We'll talk soon."

CHAPTER TEN — *Charlie*

Sofía had taken León to their room to get him settled for the night. Nancy was scanning the news on her laptop.

I opened a second beer for us all. "Luis, what's your story?"

"I came to the US from Mexico in 1980. I was nineteen. I was a mojado—a wetback. My plan was to join the army and get citizenship. It was not a bad plan. It was possible to do this back then, but I needed a green card for it to happen—I didn't know that. When I showed up at the recruiting office I was accepted, or so I thought. It turns out I was recruited by a private military contractor, not the US military. I became a mercenary. Remember, I was a teenager and I barely spoke English at that time. I had no idea it was not the regular army. That happened to a lot of us.

"When I learned what happened I went to my commander. He told me I could report the company. He explained that if I did I would be discharged and deported back to Mexico. He said the company existed because the government wants a dark army to do things the regular army could not. He also said that they had been in this business for a long time and, if I stayed for my contract, I would not only get paid well, I would get a green card. He could not promise me citizenship but he could promise me a green card. So I stayed."

"They trained you, sent you places?"

"Si. I was in Iraq twice. Afghanistan three times. Pakistan. Somalia. I was even in Kosovo. It was very bad, there. A terrible place. They were all horrible places, but Kosovo was the worst for me. We abducted people. Killed people. Assassinated people. But mostly we cleaned up other's messes. We would blend in and try to look like the locals. That is why they liked recruiting guys with brown skin. Dress local and keep your head down, you can go places big white gringos cannot. Not so much of a help in Kosovo, though.

"It was a true shadow army. I had forty guys in my platoon. We had a full company of Mexicans, Guatemalans, and Salvadorans. I was the leader of my squad but personnel changed all the time. Or got killed. After a while it became just a job. I counted the days until my contract was up."

"Did they make good on their promises?"

"Oh yes, they did. I got my green card and my salary. I saved most of it when I was overseas. Five years. A hundred thousand dollars. No taxes. And I had a green card."

"So, a good decision then?"

"No, I was pretty messed up. They call it Post Traumatic Stress Disorder. It is not post traumatic stress; it is all stress, all the time. No 'post' about it. I was jumpy, depressed, could not sleep. I had nothing. No family. No job. Sure, a pocket full of money, but for what? No, it was not a good decision."

"So, what did you do?"

"I went to California. Hung out with some ex-mercenaries. Did some drugs. Got in a bit of trouble. Basically what the other guys did."

"But now you're a gardener in Phoenix? How'd that happen?"

"I met Juanita in California and we had Sofía. Juanita wanted to move away from LA and I didn't. We fought. We ended up fighting about everything. Juanita had a job, but I had no work. I was restless, impossible to live with. I was just getting high all the time and we were running out of money. So I left and signed up again. This time with the US Army. It made sense at the time."

"Wow. Same mistake again."

"Not so much the second time. Juanita and Sofía got medical benefits and I signed over most of my salary. Kept some beer money. I provided for them—that was good. Because I had a green card and experience I became a corporal. Higher pay. I stayed ten years. Ten long years. Even got a small pension when I got out. Came home maybe five times over those years. Sofía grew up without me."

"Juanita?"

"Nothing changed, Charles. I gave Juanita everything when we separated, but it was not much. I stopped sending support when Sofía was grown. Being a gardener doesn't pay much, but working with plants is a good thing for me."

"Can't you apply for citizenship?"

"Yes, I can but I do not know that I want to do this. I know that is loco but what is here for me? I do not love this country. I hate the government. If I did not have Sofía and León I might have gone back to Mexico or worse, re-enlisted."

CHAPTER ELEVEN

"Katie, I've been doing some research on-line. There's a California forum on immigration I checked out and it's really frightening what's going on down there. A lot of people are planning personal exit strategies or fighting politically. Even librarians are involved."

"How does that help your parents?"

"Well, people are making plans to get out if they have to, so that means there are ways. There's a lot of help, if my parents can find it. The main thing is that the west coast of the US is sympathetic to Dreamers and other undocumented immigrants. Canadians, too I bet. California, Oregon and Washington are considered sanctuary states. Certain cities are sanctuary cities as well"

"What does that mean?"

"Basically it means that the local cops there aren't doing the Fed's work for them. They're not asking for proof of residency when they stop someone. In Arizona, and a lot of other states, any kind of stop by a cop, even for something like a burned-out taillight, can result in them demanding that information. And if your papers aren't in order they'll hand you over to ICE. You can get deported if you're arrested for jaywalking or riding your bicycle on the sidewalk, even if you have papers, because you've technically committed a crime. In sanctuary states a driver's license is all that's asked for because the regular cops aren't enforcing immigration laws for ICE."

"So all Nancy and Charlie need to do is get to California and drive up the coast. That's great."

"Yeah, we'll text them that information. They should be fine."

CHAPTER TWELVE — *Charlie*

We woke to the sound of traffic and car doors slamming. A short time later Bobby knocked briefly and rushed into the room. He looked upset.

He spoke rapidly in Spanish to Luis who headed to the bedroom where Sofía and León were. Then Bobby turned to me.

"Charlie, something is happening. I don't know what's going on. It's like the hotel has been invaded. We have new security staff setting up checkpoints. People wearing some kind of government ID. I have to get down to the front desk and get my new ID. There are metal detectors at the main entrances. There are government vehicles everywhere—they're all black and full of people and guns. This is not about you, señor; this is about some kind of high security guest or something. We have to get you out of here right now!"

"Which way?"

"For you and Nancy the back exit is best. Get your vehicle and take it towards the trash containers. There is a small alley there. Follow it. It leads to the maintenance sheds. But, before you get to them, there's a break in the fence. Go through it. Drive slowly. The area has rough ground, maybe broken glass. Turn towards the road and try to look like you do it all the time. There is security already setting up on the road. Vamonos, Charlie."

"What about Luis and Sofía?"

"I'll handle that, señor. I'll keep them safe. Don't worry. I don't know how and I don't know when, but I'll get them out."

"No, Bobby. We won't leave them. They come with us."

Bobby turned, yelled at Luis, ran into the bedroom and grabbed the baby. He brought León to us. "Okay. I'll bring them down. You take León and get the truck started. We'll be at the back door in a minute."

Nance picked León up and held him close. She looked at Sofía. Sofía met her eyes for a long second and turned back into the bedroom as we left the suite. As we were getting into the truck a man in a black uniform came out of the back entrance.

"Sir. Please stop. Have you been cleared by the front desk?"

"If you mean, have I checked out? Yes. We checked out much earlier but didn't want to leave until the baby woke up. Why? They want me to check out again?"

"No, sir. We're securing the hotel for government purposes and everyone has to be checked for security reasons, sir."

"Even those who are already checked out?"

He looked pointedly at the plates on the truck. "You're leaving right now, sir? You aren't scheduled to return?"

"Nope. It's been great but I've had enough of Arizona, thank you. Time to go home."

"Okay, then, sir. Please leave directly. Please make sure I don't see you again, sir. No offense."

He strode past and continued his rounds. The back of him was a message. He'd return shortly and I'd better be out of there by then. I waited until he turned the corner and then I started the truck. Nance sat in the back seat holding León. We waited. Time seemed to stop. I couldn't stall much longer. It was an excruciating wait. After a few more minutes I was about to leave, inching the wheels forward, when I saw the exit door open and Sofía and Luis emerge. I pulled up, they jumped in and then Bobby appeared at my window.

"Bobby, I was spotted by a government security guy. He's coming back. He might see me take the maintenance road. Can you go around the corner and, if you see him, direct his attention somewhere else? I need a few minutes to disappear."

Bobby moved like a cat. He was around the corner and on mission faster than I could get the truck moving. I headed for the trash containers. They weren't high enough to hide me from the security guy but they made our presence a little less noticeable. After a bit I saw the break in the fence and took the truck slowly through it. We were on a building lot. It had been cleared but not serviced. Somebody had dumped trash. There was a shopping cart lying on its side. Nature was trying to reclaim the property with some dry looking bushes. We stood out like Dennis Rodman in North Korea.

As I approached the road, I saw a military Humvee heading towards the hotel entrance. The driver looked over at us, obviously curious about what we were doing driving through the empty lot. I gave him a patriotic nod. He kept going. Don't ask me what a patriotic nod is, but I gave one *and* it worked.

We turned up Hayden with the intention of retracing our route to get back to the 101. That plan changed as we neared the sports complex. The stands and fields had been taken over by government forces and they were a clear and present danger as we approached the turn onto Princess. So I kept going instead. Stayed on the Greenway Hayden Loop until I got to North Scottsdale, turned right and we joined the 101 just past the Penske Racing museum.

"That was way too close, Luis. What took you so long at the hotel?"

"We had to help Bobby break the plumbing. He was already late for reporting in and he needed to have an excuse. We needed to break a pipe and leak some water to make his story *hold* water. It's always about water down here, Charles. It is life in the desert."

Sofía and Nancy smiled. I was getting concerned that Luis was developing a sense of humor. But just at that moment, Luis' phone rang.

"I think you'd better put your gringo friend on the line." Luis handed it to me.

"Hello, Terry."

"Guess what I found?"

"Yeah, I knew you would. I guess you want the long version now."

"You got that right, asshole. I trusted you. I'm going to fucking hunt you down like a dog. I don't care what nice shit you did for Luis and Sofía, you're mine."

"Terry, Terry. Relax. Your trust was warranted. Mostly. Just listen. You called, right? You want to listen, right? So, listen already."

"Okay. But, know this you lying prick; if one thing doesn't sound right I'm alerting every cop in the state to arrest your ass. I swear to God. I already know some things you don't know I know, so I suggest that you tell the truth, the whole truth and, so help me God, don't you leave anything out."

So I told him everything. I even told him I knew who'd turned us in.

"How'd you know that?"

"My friend, Steve, had Garth and Bambi check on his house now and then. I think they had a key. No one else in the community knew we were there except some old Mormon guy up the way who was lonely and sad. And yet two guys show up, grab Nance and look for me. They had no worries about dogs or about there being more than two old people to deal with. They didn't even seem to have a vehicle so they must've been dropped off and were planning on taking ours. They could only get that information from one source."

"You got that right. That couple already filed for their cut of the bounty. Double rates 'cause you're murderers."

"Murder *suspects*, Terry. I told you it was self defense. Think about it. They had guns. I had a putter. We lived there, they broke in.

I'll bet they're known to the police. My guess is you know who they are. You know I'm telling the truth."

"Let's pretend for a minute that I believe you. That doesn't change anything. I'm not the judge. I bring you in and let others decide whether to believe you or not. What choice do I have? The neighbors have filed an incident report. I can't sit on it."

"I know. Do what you gotta do, Terry. When you stopped us up on Superstition I hoped it wouldn't come to this. I told Luis that when I got back to Canada I was going to call and tell you everything."

"Now I'm not believing you again."

"Okay. Maybe this will help. There were two guns. Both intruders had one. I gave you the murder weapon—I mean the self defense weapon. I didn't give you the second gun. If it helps, I'll leave it where you can find it. I honestly don't see how it can help but, if you want it, it's yours."

"I'm not going to go to some place in the middle of the desert and look behind a cactus to find a gun. I do believe you. But know this—that gun will lead you to more trouble than solution. Trust me. You don't want to have it."

"I tend to agree. We almost got caught by ICE this morning and, had they found the gun, I'd probably have been sent to Guantanamo by now."

"ICE is rounding up people in California?"

"No. We spent the night in Scottsdale. The Desert Oasis Resort. Nice place. But in the morning ICE was on the scene in a big way. We were lucky to get out. There are hundreds of ICE agents at the sports complex. And they were taking over the hotel when we left."

"How'd you get a room there? They have to report you."

"Another long story, Terry. I'll tell you when we get back to Canada."

"I have to put out an APB. You know I do."

"Of course. No problem. We were last seen on the Superstition Freeway. I told you when you checked us out that we were heading east, didn't I? I think I did. That was our plan at the time, anyway. Well, one of our plans. Terry, our problem is not your problem. Do the right thing. That's all. Do what you have to. I'm okay with that."

"Sofía good?"

"Yeah. She and León are remarkably good. The kid's a doll. You want me to say something to her?"

"No, just wondered. Luis is good if Sofía is good. And I'm good if they're good. Just asking. And get rid of that fucking gun, man. Damn it. Okay, I saw you heading east on the Superstition Freeway. But that's fucking it. Get the hell out of Arizona and get the hell out today."

"Will do, Terry. And shall I tell Sofía you're more than interested in her well being?"

"You shut the hell up. Goddamn Canadians."

CHAPTER THIRTEEN

"Aba, I bin thinkin'. You want Sofía, she don' want you."

"You loco, man? You think I don' know she don' love me, man? I know that. I fucking hate it but it's true, vato. She loved the drogs, man. She loved them, not me. I could let her go, you know I could. But I got a kid now. I'm a father now. And I wanna be a good papa. All that father baseball shit. I want some of that. Never had that as a kid, man. My old man was killed by the army in El Salvador. Poor, fucking dirt farmer and they raid us and kill him . . . What the fuck for, man? What the fuck for?"

"So, ya wanna do somethin' for the kid?"

"Yeah. For the fuckin' kid, man. If the mama comes along too, that's okay, but it's really for the kid.

"Well . . . Sofía phoned me. Said they're with some gringos heading north out of Phoenix and they're tryin' to get to California. She said she was scared, man. Seems the gringos offed a couple of vigilantes to get away. That's some heavy shit, man."

"Why she talkin' to you? What the fuck. Why you, Miguel, eh?

"She calls, man. She asks about you."

"You fucking liar! You said she hates me, man. How can she hate me if she be callin'?

"She calls me, Aba. Not you. She says she's never comin' back, man. She just wants to check. See if you still alive and shit. I didn't want you to get your hopes up. Anyway, fuckin' Luis, man, he never gonna let you see her. He'll kill you, man. You know that."

"That ol' asshole. Don't he know I saved her ass? I mean, she had it bad, man. I saved her, you know it. Was me who got her off the junk. You know that. This is a bad business but it was through dealin' I met her. I met my girl selling junk . . . man that is fucked up. That is so fucked up. I gotta set this right, somehow."

"Right now your little boy is ridin' with armed gringos who killed some dudes. All we know is they headed this way. I dunno, man . . . how you set that right?"

They were interrupted by a knock at the door. After a slight pause, another one, harder this time.

"Aba! I know you're in there. Rodriguez. Open up!"

"Miguel, see if he's alone."

Miguel got up from the couch and opened the door. He stepped aside when he saw only one cop. Rodriguez took it as an invitation to enter. Miguel took a seat off to the side, watching. He assumed the persona he always did around police, strangers, other banditos. He was perceived as Aba's assistant, a bit simple, even stupid. And he preferred it that way.

"Relax, Aba. No hassle. Some dudes downtown want to ask you some questions."

"I don't know nothin'."

"Rodriguez laughed out loud. "Fuck, man. You must know something about something. How the fuck d'ya get to be *the* pusher man in Compton knowing nothing?"

"If you ain't arresting me, Rodriguez, what the fuck you want?"

"I told ya, man. Some dudes wearing black suits and flashing government ID think you might know something. Some computer got your name and they want to talk to you."

"'Bout what?"

"I dunno. They don't tell me. But I heard something about your old lady."

"I'm not married. Wrong guy!"

"No shit? But, you got a kid, right? Your name shows up as the father of some kid and that kid is with a woman the Feds are looking for, I'm guessing. They figure you might know something, being the father and all."

Aba thought fast. The Feds could find Sofía easier than he could. Plus they already knew he was the father. He gives them Sofía and demands to take care of his son.

"I might know something. I don't know what, but I'll go with you. Two conditions."

Rodriguez laughed again. "You're hardly in a position to negotiate, Aba. There are at least two warrants out for you and I can easily call in a couple of cars, claiming you resisted. Don't make me get creative, man. Just come in and stop with all that shit."

"First, you gotta bring me back here after. Fucking LAPD picks you up and tells you to take the bus home, man. That's fucked up. No wonder everyone hates your fucking guts."

"Okay, I'll give you a ride back. Now, let's go."

"Second condition. I get the kid. If you arrest Sofía, I get my son. Deal?"

"The judge decides that. Probably they'll put the kid in care if it comes to that. You're hardly a good role model, Aba. Not even for a drug dealer. You're a fucking low-life selfish prick spreading misery and fear in your own motherfucking neighborhood. Who's going to give you a kid? You must be crazy."

"Then I don' know nothin'. Nothin'! I ain't goin' downtown. Eat shit and die, Rodriguez."

Rodriguez wanted to get Aba downtown. He'd acted pretty confident that he could track down a dealer in the area and get him in voluntarily. He'd practically swaggered when he said it. He wanted to impress the suits and this was his chance.

"You got any judgments or shit making you stay away from the mother or child?"

Aba shook his head.

"The mama hate you or fear you?"

"She don' love me, man, but she knows I love my kid. I think she'd give 'im up to me for a while. If she think she goin' down, she gonna try an' let me keep 'im."

"Anybody related to her or you in LA who could take the kid?"

Aba thought of Luis. But, if Sofía got arrested, so would Luis, so he kept that to himself.

"No, man. Jus' me and Sofía and the kid. Only people she knows are junksluts and shit. She got no one but me."

"I can't make any promises, Aba, but if you cooperate and I have a chance to put in a word, I will. I don't like the child custody people one bit. Kids get eaten up in that system. "How old is he?"

"Almost two. His name is León."

"Don't get your hopes up, father-of-the-year. I can't see the judge giving up a two year old that easy. But like I say, I'll do what I can."

Aba got up from the bed, crossed the floor to Miguel and whispered something. Then he walked out. Rodriguez followed but didn't bother to look at Miguel. After a moment, Miguel dialed Sofía's cell.

CHAPTER FOURTEEN

"So, Aba, spill. What do you know?"

Aba sat at a simple table covered in stainless steel in a room like every other interrogation room he'd ever been in. Hard chairs, harsh lights, stupid mirrored wall. But no cuffs this time. Aba wasn't impressed.

"Don't I get a coffee or sump'n? I mean, I'm a guest, right? Doin' my fuckin' civic duty. Don' you treat a good citizen better than this shit?"

There were three people in the room. Aba, the suit and Rodriguez. The suit stood off to one side. So far, this was in Rodriguez' hands.

"Aba, I ain't going to lie to you, man. We appreciate you being here, we really do. We love ya, man. But, here's the deal, you know something and you gotta tell us. Because, if you don't, you go from being a beloved citizen to being an accomplice. Or maybe obstructing justice.

"If that happens I'll have to step aside and introduce you to Mr. Suit. He swings more weight than I do. These guys can disappear you, man. You wanna go with the FBI? Or keep it in the family? So, what've you got?"

Aba knew there was going to be a double cross when he agreed to come in and this was it. Cooperate or get implicated. Bastards. Still, Rodriguez normally kept his word and he'd said he'd help get Aba his son. Time to sing.

"Sofía called Miguel. She's not allowed to talk to me. Not because of no judge or nothing. Her father hates my guts. Thinks I hooked her up. I didn't. I saved her sorry junky ass. I loved the bitch. I was good to her."

"Yeah. Great. So that's what love has to do with it. I get it. But, like, so what? Sofía calls Miguel to what? Ask about you?"

"That's right. To ask about me, man. She asks about me."

"Touching. And that's it? How's Aba doing? She calls and asks how Aba is doing? You expect me to believe that shit?"

Aba was embarrassed. Rodriguez was right. So what if her padre forbid her to talk to him? Why didn't she just phone when he wasn't around? Why the hell was Sofía calling Miguel, anyway?

Aba just sat there. Rodriguez sensed that the focus of the interrogation had gone sideways and he had to get it back.

"So, how did you know she was traveling with gringos?"

"Miguel told me."

Rodriguez was sweating now. "You told me she'd called and said she was riding with gringos who killed two guys. Is that right?"

"Yeah." Aba wasn't feeling like cooperating. Something was missing . . . he had to think.

Rodriguez shifted topics. "What are they driving, Aba? Who's in the car?"

"How the fuck should I know? She talked to Miguel. I just told ya."

Rodriguez knew he'd blown it. He stood up, stepped aside and gestured to the suit.

"Aba, I'm Agent Henry. As you know, I'm with the FBI. We have reason to believe that your ex-common-law wife, Sofía, the mother of your son León, is being transported across state lines from Arizona to California by suspects wanted in the murder of two men in Phoenix. Did you know that?"

"Yeah. Kinda."

"We also have reason to believe that they're coming to Los Angeles. We assume it's to see you. Could the reason be Miguel? Could she be coming to see Miguel instead of you, Aba?"

Aba struggled to keep his temper. He was practically exploding inside with the very same questions and the answers threatened to make him crazy. He remained silent and simply gripped the chair.

Interrogators know when a question has struck a nerve. That one had. It was time to dial it back. "Maybe she doesn't have a choice, Aba? Maybe she's been taken against her will. Maybe her father made her come or maybe the suspects did. Could that be it?"

Aba was so pumped with rage he almost didn't hear what Henry said but after a moment he realized that made more sense. Sofía had no choice. She was taken against her will. That had to be it. She wasn't coming to see Miguel. That was insane. Luis made her come. This was all Luis' fault.

"Yeah, man. Sofía's got no control, man. She got no power. She's a Dreamer, right? No papers, no card, nothin'. Luis protects her, right? I used to. Luis has the power, man. If he says run, they run. It's Luis pulling the strings, man."

"Good. Thanks Aba. That helps. But we got nothing on a Luis Mendez. It's like the guy lived his whole life out of sight, you know? I mean, how'd this guy come to America? When? We got no intel on this guy. Do you know anything about him?"

"Luis is a tough guy, man. I don' mess with Luis. No one messes with Luis. He was a soldier. Peoples say he was a merc, man. He's been in Iraq and shit."

"How do you know this?"

"That's the word on the street, I guess. Sofía said something . . . I dunno . . . I just know when Luis came to find Sofía, when he learned she was shooting up, he went wherever he wanted to go and he did whatever he needed to. He left some real hard asses hurtin'. I respect the dude, man, he real tough."

"So, he found Sofía? He found her with you?"

"Yeah, he found us after León was born. Not a happy abuelo, dude."

"So, what happened?"

"He took 'em. He just walked in and took 'em both. I didn't stop him. He would've killed me, man. Took 'em both back to Arizona."

"So, why are they coming back to LA?"

"Vigilantes, man. What the fuck? You so stupid you don't know that vigilantes are crawling all over Arizona looking to catch anyone with dark skin and turn 'em in for a bounty? What the fuck did you think would happen when you come down on folks like that?"

"So, you think the gringos they're with are vigilantes?"

"You got shit for brains? They runnin' *from* vigilantes. If they was vigilantes, they woulda turned Luis and Sofía in for the bounty. No, asshole, they runnin' from the fuckin' vigilantes, the fuckin' police, ICE and just about every fuckin' red-neck bastard and white guy in a suit they see. I get it. I live the same way, man."

"Miguel said the FBI is looking for me," Sofía said very softly, in Spanish, to Luis.

"I told you not to talk to Aba, Sofía. Or Miguel. They are no good. Why is the FBI looking for you and how does he know that?"

"It's my fault. I told Miguel we were with an old white couple who killed some vigilantes. He must have mentioned it to someone. I'm sorry, papa. I didn't know that would happen."

Luis briefed me and we decided that there was nothing we could do about it at this point.

"We're on highway 40. Let's just get out of Arizona. At least that'll cut down the vigilante threat."

"Some."

"What do you mean, 'some', Luis?"

"Registered bounty hunters can cross state lines. I doubt that many of the vigilantes would, but a registered guy might. It depends on the bounty."

"Well, we're still considered a two hundred dollar bounty, right?"

"Maybe not. If you are both wanted for murder, a bounty hunter would get the extra two hundred for you and Nancy. Sofía and I could be arrested as accessories. With the four of us at four hundred each, that is sixteen hundred, plus little León at two hundred. It is getting to be a big number."

After a moment spent considering Luis' encouraging words, I decided I should fill him in about the gun I still had in my possession.

"Luis, I have another gun."

"I know. H&K .45. Same as the other one. It is stored between your seat and the console."

"How'd you know?"

"I am not stupid, Charles. Two vigilantes means two guns. Terry took one of them. You had one left. Duh."

"I have a full clip and a little bag of ammo, too."

"A little bag?"

Charlie handed the bag, the clip and the gun to Luis.

"Better you should have it. I don't even know how to load it."

"Well, for a gun-controlled Canadian senior citizen collecting his old age pension, your kill ratio is off the charts, Charles."

* * * * *

"Ben, I need you to get a burner phone or one that's not traceable to you."

"*What? Why?*"

"We're running from the FBI. It's only a matter of time before they locate you. They may have already. Get the new phone, message me the number from it, and I'll call you on it from a pay phone, or a burner if we can get one. We'll use our normal phones to send misleading messages. I'll call you, say something that'll send them in the wrong direction, and hang up. Five minutes later, I'll call you on the burner phone."

"That's ridiculous."

"You're the one who's paranoid about all this crap. That's why I know about it in the first place. And I'd hate for you to be implicated. It's really important to do this right away."

"You need to keep me and Katie informed. Why is the FBI involved? I thought this was an immigration problem."

"It's complicated. And I'm sorry, Ben, we're going to call you only when we have to. Maybe once or twice to throw them off. You'll have to get used to hearing nothing."

"Okay, no news is good news."

"That's odd, Charles."

"What?"

"That big eighteen wheeler we just passed. The truck and trailer. It is really old. And it was parked on the side of the road with three guys sitting in the front seat. Does that not seem odd to you?"

"Is it like the one up ahead that's just pulling onto the highway?"

"Not pulling on—pulling *across*! This does not look good. We're going to be trapped between them."

I drew the Avalanche to a stop. Luis, Nancy and I watched while the truck ahead jockeyed into position, blocking the highway. If there was any way to get around it wasn't evident, and worse, the truck moving out revealed a couple of jacked up pickup trucks on the side of the road facing us. This was planned. Interstate 40 was totally blocked just a few miles west of Yucca, Arizona. Vigilantes.

I looked to back up and turn around but Luis said, "Do not bother. The first truck is doing the same thing. They are blocking the highway, too. We are boxed in."

The trucks had chosen a good spot to set up the roadblock. The edge of the highway was mostly lined with metal or concrete barriers that stopped vehicles from crossing the median or going off the road. The section they had chosen was about a thousand feet long, more than half of which was a bridge under which railroad tracks ran. The drop was enough to kill anyone in a vehicle, even if they could bust through the walls or dividers. The only way out of this was to head across the median to the other side of the highway, but the median was steep, and most of it was barricaded as well.

I spun the truck around and headed back towards the first semi where three guys were now getting out of the cab. I accelerated hard.

"Charlie, what are you doing?" Nancy shrieked. "The road's blocked. They're getting out. They've got guns!"

At the last second, I braked hard and turned the wheel to the right. The truck's tires shrieked in protest and the smell of burning rubber filled the cab. We skidded to a halt and drew up parallel to the blockade, just about twenty feet away. All we could see was a truck and guns to our left and an empty abyss in front of us. I stomped on the gas.

"Ready, Luis?" I asked.

"Ready, Thelma."

The truck leaped forward and seemed to jump into the air. There was a second while the tires gripped the road and then a sensation of weightlessness as the vehicle seemed to float over the edge.

The incline was severe. The truck was still practically airborne when the front wheels hit the scree slope. The worst part was that the rear of the truck seemed to rise as the front fell. It felt as if we were virtually standing on our nose. My foot wasn't on the brake. I knew that to brake was to guarantee we would flip. We could pitch-pole, I thought, the term from my sailing days coming to mind for no good reason.

The front wheels hit, buried a bit, but they rolled. They rolled enough for the back of the truck to stop its somersaulting trajectory. But we were now heading quickly for some large boulders and I sensed that the front of the truck would simply stop hard against them. I yanked the wheel to the right and one tire seemed to find something to grip. But the impact and the new found traction had made the big truck bounce. Everyone inside was thrown around, including me. I almost lost control.

The momentum of the truck dictated the new trajectory. Sideways. It was still going downhill but it was at too much of an angle to continue to stay upright. I could feel it wanting to roll down the rest of the slope. Driver's side first. Once again, I yanked the wheel, this time in the direction of the lean and, even though there was a horrible clunk as the undercarriage was slammed down and dragged across some large rocks, the truck stayed on its tires. We came to a rest at the bottom with the back wheels stuck in the air. The frame was hung up on the last of the boulders.

I shifted into four wheel drive and tried to get enough traction from the front wheels to pull the truck forward. After a second or two, it was clear this wasn't working. I shifted into reverse and tried this time to use the front wheels and the weight of the truck that was on them to push the truck farther back up the rocks. It moved a few inches but protested the whole way. I then quickly shifted again into forward and tried to get a bit of momentum. It worked. The truck moved farther into the dry bottom of the median but it wasn't enough—it was still hung up.

In my rearview mirror I could see two of the vigilantes on foot heading down the slope towards us. I involuntarily pushed down harder on the accelerator and the truck jumped. Now the back two wheels were on the ground but they began to slip in some sand. I knew instantly that they'd dig themselves in and there would be no getting away. I stopped and put the truck in reverse again. Years of driving in Canadian winters had taught me to keep the vehicle moving. Any direction of movement was better than no movement at all. And spinning the wheels only makes things worse. Better to rock back and forth. Better to go backwards than just sit still.

The Avalanche did move backwards, aided by gravity and its own massive power plant. Just as I heard the back of the truck scraping on the boulders behind me. I put it in forward and surged towards solid ground. Once again the front of the truck leaped up and once again the rear wheels found the soft sand. My heart practically stopped. I wasn't going to make it.

One more time I dropped it into reverse, this time smashing backwards over the boulders a bit farther, hoping that I didn't get caught up on them again. Back into drive. The big 4x4 leaped forward and this time my fear added a bit more acceleration to the mix than I intended.

The big truck leaped and I could feel that the rear wheels weren't stopping at the same spot. At the very least, the angle of attack had changed enough to miss the soft sand and I gave it all the gas I dared. We moved forward. We were free.

"Well, we are better off than they were, Charles."

"Than who were?"

"Thelma and Louise."

CHAPTER SEVENTEEN — *Charlie*

The dry median sloped towards the rail line so I headed west, paralleling the highway. When we got to the railroad tracks it was clear that we couldn't climb up the opposite side of the median. It was steeper than what we had just come down and it would put the truck directly in the sights of the second blockade.

I turned north and followed the train tracks. For the first few yards we were hidden from view by the overhead bridge but we knew that, as soon as we passed under the roadway, we'd be seen. Worse, we didn't have much choice but to follow the tracks and the road beside them. The area was boulder strewn and at least ten or so feet below the general elevation of the desert. Better to get some distance between us and the bastards. I pushed the truck as hard as I could.

"They coming?"

Luis looked out the back window, surveying the scene unfolding on the bridge overhead. "I do not know, Charles. The pickup is heading west. They must know of an easier place to get down to the desert. And they may know where we are going."

"How can they? We don't know."

"Maybe there is no choice. Perhaps the gully forces us to follow the tracks. It looks that way."

"Yeah. How far are we from Yucca?"

"A little less than a mile. But Yucca is a ghost town."

"Well, there are a few people there," Nancy said. "I was reading up on the area. Most of the town is abandoned, but there are some residents."

"Yeah, Nance. We just missed meeting a few of them. But at least we can follow the tracks into Yucca or pretty damn close."

"Why would we want to do that?" she asked, "More vigilantes? Cops?"

"I don't think we should just keep following the train tracks. It's flat enough to head north over the desert. But I don't know the way. And I don't know if the truck can do it. It feels a bit different. We may have damaged something. And some of this ground is pretty soft."

"Charles, head into town—as soon as you can." said Luis. "There cannot be a town full of vigilantes and anyway, they cannot organize another roadblock so quickly. They chose an ideal spot back on the highway and we still got through. Just find a street where you can and head for the highway."

I saw the back of some buildings and assumed there was a street there. I pulled the Avalanche up the shallow side of the rail bed and drove through scrub brush and cactus until what passed for a street presented itself. We headed west paralleling the highway which we could occasionally glimpse. We were only a few hundred yards from it but where was an on-ramp?

Yucca wasn't one of those towns that had put imagination into naming their streets. There was first, second, third and fourth streets running east and west and they intersected a grid of avenues that went by the same designations. I found myself heading west on First Street, just before Sixth Avenue.

We paused at each avenue and had a look. It appeared that the highway was just a few blocks away so one of the side streets had to lead to an entrance ramp. It was a risky move, based on nothing but a gut feeling, but when I saw the overhead pedestrian bridge at the end of Third Avenue, I turned. Some kind of landmark is as good as any. Third took us to Frontage Road and I turned right. It had to be the way.

The vigilantes weren't stupid. They knew that their prey would try exiting Yucca. And they knew the only exit was by way of Frontage. They sat in the lot of the truck service centre just outside the main part of town. Anyone fleeing Yucca had to go that way.

We and the hunters saw each other at the same time. Their truck pulled out onto Frontage to block our way but this time they were relying on firepower rather than the single pickup truck blockade. Three armed men stood on the road, one on each side of the truck and one behind it. They weren't taking any chances. I slowed.

"Keep going," instructed Luis. "Open the back windows. They do not know how many of us there are. Which side of their truck do you think is best to get around them?"

"The road's flatter, but narrower, on the right side. And that big bastard has a telephone pole he can step behind. But, if I can get to the pole, I can make it. I like the flat side best."

"Okay, drive in that direction and put on your turn signal to indicate you are pulling over."

"Put my blinker on! What the hell for?"

"Just do it. Everyone else get down. When you are sure you can get through the gap, just slow to a stop. He should step out. I will shoot him. Then hammer it. If I miss him, duck your head and go like hell anyway. If I can, I will try for a second target."

I did as instructed. I pulled over and almost came to a stop. The big guy remained in position but the guy on the other side started to walk away from his side of the truck. He was out in the open.

I spoke softly to Luis, "The guy from the left side is coming but the big guy is still behind the pole. I may just have to hit it."

"Stay calm. Look at the left side guy but don't put your window down."

I did as he said and improvised somewhat by showing my hands as though I was surrendering. But the truck was aimed at the gap and I was ready to punch it when the big guy stepped out. Still looking left, I said, "The big guy's out. Take the shot."

Luis rose, shot twice, and struck him in his head somewhere. The guy fell backwards. I saw the small cloud of red mist where his face had just been. And I hit the accelerator. The truck jumped for the gap just as I heard more shots. Luis had crossed the back seat right over Sofía and the baby and managed to get off a third and fourth shot. The second guy jerked but remained standing. He'd been hit but I didn't see him go down.

The third guy, who had been behind the truck, had a rifle and was setting up to take aim. I held my direction for a second and then shifted the truck to the wrong lane of Frontage road. By doing that, he had to aim again. I held the truck there for two long seconds and then jumped back into the proper lane. We weren't hit. I didn't even hear a shot. By then, we were eight hundred feet out and still accelerating. I breathed a bit easier but left my foot flat on the floor, letting the big V-8 work as hard as it could.

By the time we passed Area 66 and the giant golf ball, we were doing over a hundred miles an hour and it still felt as if we were, somehow, not going fast enough.

"You can slow down now, Charles. One guy is down. I think I nicked the second guy and anyone else they have is likely back at the semis. They are not coming. The cops might come. But they are not."

"Jeez, Luis. Hitting that first guy was some shot but even getting close to that second guy was some kind of miracle."

"I just got lucky. The first guy was a big target. I took my shots at the second guy just as the truck moved."

"Not the first time you've done this, Luis."

"No, Charles. Not the first time."

CHAPTER EIGHTEEN

Washington, Henry's junior agent, reported in. "We've located them. They're getting close to crossing into California, sir. They shot two guys in Yucca. Probably vigilantes, according to the Highway Patrol. One's dead. One's in hospital. Looks like they're headed toward Barstow."

"Other than the local sheriff's office, do we have any assets there?"

"No, and it's a small detachment in Barstow. Just six or so officers per shift and a lot of territory to cover. They can be supplemented by the Highway Patrol and the BLM rangers, if we request it. There are DoD police at Fort Irwin, but generally they're limited to their jurisdiction. There's no real force to ensure a safe arrest, especially at this point. By the time we finish this conversation, sir, they may have already gone through Barstow. It isn't that big."

"Okay, then let's plan around picking them up when they get to LA. The tail's still with Aba?"

"Yes."

"We need to follow Miguel, too."

"All our assets are deployed, sir. We could ask LAPD."

"No. For now let's hope Aba and Miguel stay together. Tell the tail to let us know if they split up. And tell Rodriguez what we're up to. He might still be useful to us, so we'll liaise."

"Sir, Barstow's only two hours away from here. If we're going to try to take them here, shouldn't we get ready?"

"No, I don't want to take agents from other assignments just yet. Don't forget, they're coming here for a reason. They could've run north, which is what I would've done. But, no, they're coming here and we just have to monitor them and take them when we know a bit more about what they're up to."

CHAPTER NINETEEN — *Dale*

I slowly eased myself out of the low Cadillac limousine and stretched. It always feels good to be able to get out and stand up straight, especially when you're as tall as I am. It'd been a long hard day and not all of my muscles and bones felt quite right, even after a stretch and a few steps. Being a limousine driver is harder than it looks.

The car belongs to Ideal Limo Service in Phoenix. I live almost an hour south in Picacho, just north of Tucson, on I-10. My beaten-up old double-wide is good enough for me and my cat, Rufus, so long as the television, the fridge and the air conditioner are working. It can get hot in Picacho.

At sixty-five I don't really want to work any more but I've got bills that my pension doesn't cover. Rufus likes to eat. I have a shooting habit I have to feed. I need the money. I'm lucky to have the job, and especially lucky that I can drive the car home. I pay towards the extra gas, but only a token amount. Of course, working for eleven dollars an hour is only token wages, so it still works out in favor of the company. Always does. This is America, after all.

America has gone all to hell. Everyone says it. Even the news says so. The corporations rip everybody off, even the banks cheat, everybody is some kind of crook and drugs are the main industry in small town USA nowadays. No one makes anything anymore. They just buy it from Walmart.

The real problem, I know for a fact, is the immigrants. They come in with their anti-Christian values, their lack of good morals, their hatred of us white people. But they still love American money. They get all the jobs and all the benefits. They lie and they cheat. They steal and sell drugs. And, if that doesn't work, the bastards become terrorists. Immigrants are ruining the country and it's plain for anyone to see. Hell, I drive past Eloy twice a day and the place is jammed with illegals and they're just the tip of the iceberg.

I'm no racist—I just hate immigrants. Ever since the US went soft on immigration, the country's been going downhill. That's what Breitbart says. That's what Rush says. And Fox. And anyone can see it's all true. We all know it, but until Trump, no one was doing a thing about it. The thing that really pisses me off is seeing all the Mexicans in the local hospitals getting free medical care, but when my wife needed treatment we couldn't afford it. That was ten years ago and it's only been getting worse since then. As far as I'm concerned, immigrants killed my wife. It's that simple.

As a rule, I'm not into politics. I used to say, "I follow the Diamondbacks, not politics." But Trump is different. Trump promised to 'Make America Great Again'. I have no idea how any one person can make our country great again but, if anyone can, it'll be the president. I voted for Trump because I believe he can do it.

When the immigration crackdown started, I knew it was the president's decision. I didn't hear it was a presidential order, but I didn't have to. Immigration has been getting tougher on Mexicans and Muslims ever since President Trump came into office. Of course he ordered the crackdown. He had to. The place is overrun with foreigners. And Muslims are the worst.

Plus, the crackdown's been good for business. I've been working ten and twelve hour days, for the last few weeks, driving non-Americans to the airport. I was wondering why so many were leaving but, when the crackdown was announced, I knew. They must have known it was coming.

The other night I stopped at C4 Tactical for a little pressure release from driving all day. I stop there all the time to shoot and hang out with the regulars. Sometimes I have a beer and a steak dinner across the street at the Tumbleweed Cafe.

That night I met up with Early and Lyle at the C4. I don't like them much, but they know their guns, and they look up to me because I'm a better shot. We're not friends, but they often show up when I'm at the range, and the three of us end up going to eat together. That night, during dinner, I ended up liking them even less than before.

"We gonna have us some fun, tomorrow eh, Lyle. Hey, Dale? You in?"

"In what?"

"Ain't you heard? You know about the immigration crackdown? Well, Corrections has a contract to take in anyone who hasn't registered. That's more or less anybody, Dale. You can haul in anyone you want."

"That can't be right. Don't you need a badge or something to take someone in?"

"No badge. Don't even need a bounty hunters' license. When you bring in your first detainee–that's what they call 'em–you just sign a paper. You know a private company runs the prisons, right? They process the fugitive and you get your bounty later. They said that anyone without the proper papers can be hauled in for a bounty. It's a quick two hundred bucks a head.

"But listen to this, Dale. How's a guy gonna know who has the proper papers? So, that means a lotta bounties are gonna be paid for spics and shit who actually have papers but ain't carrying 'em. If they got 'em with them, you can't take 'em in. But even if you know they got papers, but they can't produce 'em, they can be hauled in. They should have the stamped cards with 'em is what Immigration figures, I guess."

I was curious about all this. "Where do you take them?"

"Around here, the easiest place is Eloy. They're taking 'em there and at the ICE office downtown. They said they're settin' up another place in Scottsdale."

"So, you're telling me that if Tia over there at the ammo counter doesn't have her green card stamped, I can walk over, arrest her, and take her in?"

"That's what they told us at Corrections." Early turned in his chair to face in the direction of the counter where Tia worked. He yelled, "Hey, Tia! You got your green card with you?"

Tia slowly turned, picked up her purse and pulled out her wallet. She held it up and, flipping it open like a cop, showed us her ID. All three of us laughed out loud and Early turned back as Tia called, "Hey, Early. You got yours?"

I laughed even harder, but Early and Lyle didn't like the comeback. "Fucking bitch. We be born and raised our whole lives here. We're American through and through—pure patriots, bitch."

And that's exactly why I don't like Early or his brother. Tia obeys the rules. She does a good job. Tia's all right. And even though immigrants are destroying the country, it isn't immigrants like her. She works long hard hours for little money, just like us. I hate Mexicans, but not Tia.

"That's it for me, fellas. I'm outta here. Long day today and even longer day tomorrow. Gotta get home and feed Rufus."

* * * * *

The talk about being a bounty hunter got me thinking. I'm a pretty tough guy. And an excellent shot. At my age, I've lost a bit in the way of hand eye coordination, reaction time, and even strength, not to mention eyesight, but I was a Ranger for six years. I was well trained. I've been in battle. I can shoot to kill if I have to.

I have to wear glasses to read now, but I can see to shoot. And, more to the point, I have a permit to carry. I have my gun with me at all times. It's a Taurus .357 magnum with a six inch barrel. I can still put a tight grouping in a target from a hundred feet. Given a bit of time, I'm good to two hundred feet. No one will mess with me and, if they do, they'll regret it.

Most Mexicans I know, like Tia, have green cards. I guess those who don't have the right papers will go back across the border, driving their car, or taking the bus. But many Mexicans are going to be unprepared. There are going to be a lot of uninformed ones hiding out or heading south about now. I'm sure of that.

A few hundred extra dollars in my pocket would go a long way. I could likely pick up some illegals on my way home tomorrow night if I gave it some thought. It wasn't much of a plan, but I'd definitely keep my eyes and ears open. I knew of a few itinerant worker camps down my way, but the pecans had been harvested already. Still, some workers might be hanging around. I might take a cruise through one of the camps, just to see.

And that's how I became a vigilante.

CHAPTER TWENTY — *Charlie*

We drove for a while in silence. As my eyes flicked over the instrument panel I saw that a light was on. "Something's wrong with the truck."

"What do you think it is?" Nancy sounded concerned.

"Don't know. The check engine light's on but the temperature and oil are okay. The truck seems a bit off, but nothing I can actually put my finger on. Probably some stupid bloody sensor. It's basically running okay. Maybe there's a bit of a wobble in the passenger side front wheel. If I stay at the speed limit it's all right, though."

"What do you want to do?"

"Let's get to Barstow and throw a scope on it. Look at the wheels and the undercarriage while we're at it. Maybe swap over the spare if the wheel seems damaged. Some of the pressure's off now that we're in California."

I drove the truck into Jake's Automotive and reported back. "They need a few hours to get a chance to look at it, which is crap. Throwing the computer on it takes two minutes. But, it doesn't matter, I'm pretty sure something is wrong with the front end or the right front wheel anyway. They need to put it on the hoist and look at that. I told them the light was of lesser importance. We may as well check in at the Barstow Lodge over there. Looks like we're going to be here overnight."

Luis and Sofía took two rooms. We took one more. All in a row. All on ground level. I had the foresight to take all our gear out of the back of the truck. Sometimes you just know things are going to go sideways, but you don't know how or when.

* * * * *

"I have to go."

Sofía hung up and tucked her phone away just as Luis came into her room.

Miguel was relieved. He'd had no choice but to promise to have things right for her. At least they weren't going to arrive in LA today. With luck, the damn truck would be out of commission for a couple of days.

He just didn't want her to arrive yet. He still had to deal with Aba and he could use more time. Miguel absentmindedly picked up one of the guns. There were always guns. Aba had half a dozen. He had three. The house they sold out of maybe had another six, not including the two shotguns at the front and back doors. Plus there was at least one gun in each of their vehicles of a fleet of ten or so.

Compton was the hub for Aba's business in LA and the drugs came in by air using the small, but very busy, Compton/Woodley airport. From there, they used everything from cars to buses, from the metro to bicycles, as well as the extensive freeway system. Aba had an efficient distribution network to get the stuff around LA. FedEx couldn't do better.

A successful drug operation also had to mix things up and Aba and his outfit were always changing up cars and storefronts and their distribution centers, for their coming and going army of street dealers. Basically, the only thing that had remained the same, since Miguel joined up three years prior, was their storage depot at the airport and his and Aba's apartments. Aba said he had to keep a high street profile so his crib was well known and admired. But nothing remained a secret long in Compton. Just about everyone knew where Miguel lived, too.

Everyone knew why they were there, as well. Both of them being on 156th street meant that getting to and from the airport was easy. They could see their mule flights land. Aba was closer to South Central Avenue and Miguel was closer to South Willington, but they were just a couple of blocks apart. And each came and went from each other's place like family. When Sofía arrived, Aba would know. Demonios, when pizza delivery arrived, Aba would know.

* * * * *

"Charlie, I left the phone in the truck. I'm going to get it."

Nancy walked from the Barstow Lodge over to the auto repair shop, a few hundred yards away. Jake, the owner, was standing outside. He wasn't looking in her direction. She could see that he was on the phone and looking directly at the plates on our truck. She didn't like the feeling that gave her. She ducked behind a concrete overpass support and stayed there until he was finished. Then she waited a few more minutes and went in to ask for the keys.

After retrieving the phone she returned the keys and engaged in some chit chat about the weather, casually mentioning what a dump the Barstow Lodge was. Jake laughed, and off she went. She continued down the street well past the Hertz car rental office which was on the opposite side. Making sure no one noticed, she crossed the street, backtracked behind some parked cars and went in and rented a van.

She drove back past Jake's and saw that the truck was still sitting in the lot. They didn't seem to be in a hurry to fix it, or even have a look at it. She now sensed that this might be intentional.

"Charlie, we've got to leave right away."

"The truck done already?"

"Nope, I'll explain later. I'll get our bags and you get Luis and Sofía. Hurry! We have the blue Chrysler minivan right out front. Don't bother checking out. Leave the lights on. And the television."

"What's going on?"

"Sweetie, you're going to have to just do it."

Luis and Sofía joined us out front in the van. As Nancy began driving out of town she explained what she'd seen. Everyone agreed that leaving was the right move.

"Did you have a problem renting the van?" I asked.

"No, I got the impression this van had been a one-way rental from LA and they were glad to see it go back. The girl at the desk didn't even check my ID. I put my wallet on the counter but I filled in the number myself. She barely glanced at it."

"Either she doesn't know about the ICE crackdown, doesn't care, or maybe she didn't even notice your Canadian license. Whatever, that's good."

"My guess is Hertz is no longer number one," Luis commented.

CHAPTER TWENTY-ONE

"Agent Henry, we're getting reports of increased activity at Aba's place. A few cars have arrived and a few heavies are in with Aba right now. It could be routine but the timing seems a little unusual."

"Any of the guys look familiar? Have you run the plates?"

"Yes sir, the owners of the cars have records. But everyone in Compton has a record so that doesn't mean much. They don't appear to be Aba's regulars, though. We think they're independents."

Henry called to update Rodriguez.

Rodriguez told him, "Aba has a lot of crew and I know most of them. I don't think the guys you're listing are part of his organization. I know Lil' Loco from my time over in Bell Gardens. He's a heavy hitter—an enforcer."

"So, Aba is bringing in outsiders? In broad daylight? For what?"

"Aba doesn't care who sees what's going down on his turf. That's how he operates. No such thing as bad publicity for him. He's seriously macho and unquestionably crazy as shit. Why he's doing this is anybody's guess."

"My guess is Miguel."

"Bullshit, man. Miguel's no threat. Aba could take Miguel all by himself. He doesn't need help for that."

"He would if he figured Miguel was laying a trap for him. If he thought Miguel was ready to take over."

"You're right. He just might think that, especially after you pretty much suggested to his face that Miguel was seeing his woman."

"Where to, sir?"

"Airport."

"You in a hurry?"

"Kinda. I was vacationing. I've been coming down here for years. Seems I was supposed to check in with Immigration. I didn't know. Now they got vigilantes out looking for people like me. I'm not so much in a hurry as I am worried about dickheads with guns."

"Why didn't you check in? It's the law."

"Just didn't know about it. As I said, I come every year and I never had to do this before. I just found out this morning. Playing golf. Guy I play with is a Fed. He asked me if I'd checked in. When I said no, he said, "Don't finish the round. Get yourself out of state. Go now." So I did. I was on the course less than an hour ago."

"*I'm* a vigilante."

"You're joking? Right?"

"Nope. Got my .357 under the seat. I could take you in. It's legal."

My passenger fell back in his seat. His features sagged. He looked out the window.

"May as well. I'm putting my place up for sale, anyway. I've had enough of this stupid country. The people are fine but the government is getting fucking crazy. Go ahead, you bastard. Take me in. Get your bounty. Just leave the fucking gun where it is. I sure as hell don't need to get shot over this bullshit."

"Tell you what. I get a two hundred dollar bounty for turning you in. You pay that and I look the other way. Deal?"

The Canadian looked at me and burst out laughing. "Fine. You have a deal. I should've known money would fix this. Land of the free it ain't."

"You can pay me for the fare and the get outta jail card, man. This is gonna be a good day."

And it was. In fact, it was such a good day that I was disappointed if I picked up a fare to the airport who wasn't trying to run from the crackdown. I got used to shaking people down real quick. Actually, I figured, it wasn't two hundred bucks since most people tipped me a twenty and, of course, they didn't do that after they paid to stay free. Still, I netted over six hundred dollars before noon and had yet to pull my gun out.

By ten o'clock that night I'd put in fourteen straight hours and even the extra cash couldn't help me stay awake. I was running way over time and dispatch kept reminding me to quit. Finally, I reported in that I was headed home.

I got on I-10 and headed south. As I got closer to the steakhouse I figured I'd have to stop and eat. I was famished and maybe a good dinner would give me some energy. One thing for sure, I wasn't having a beer. This had to be a quick stop. At the last minute, I decided to skip the steak and grab a burger from the In-N-Out. Easier. Faster.

I took the West Ray Road exit, headed east and turned left into the mall. Just west of the In-N-Out is the Sandhill Mexican Grill. I was about to turn right when I caught sight of some sort of fight over at the Grill. There were some pickup trucks parked on the east side of the building and a lot of shouting going on at the front. I turned left instead and cut the lights. The big black limo crept quietly towards the front parking area, lost in the shadows.

There were two big guys with baseball bats and two more with shotguns. They were threatening a large group of customers at the front of the restaurant. Seems the altercation was between some beefy white guys and a Mexican family. I stayed back and watched with the window down.

"Show us your fucking green cards or we're fucking taking you in!"

"Fuck you, motherfucker, we ain't showin' you nothin'. Get back in your trucks, Anglos, or there gonna be blood spilt tonight!"

I could see that this was quickly getting out of hand. Some of the women and children were running back into the restaurant and, worse, some Mexican males were heading for their cars. I knew they weren't leaving. Someone was going to get hurt, if not killed.

Without thinking, I accelerated hard and brought the big limousine right between the white guys and the crowd out front of the restaurant. I jumped out with my .357 in hand, put a shot in the air to get everyone's attention, and then pointed the barrel straight at the first guy with a shotgun.

"Drop it. *Now.*"

The big guy slowly lowered the shotgun and I hissed, "I said drop it and I said now. You have one second."

The gun clattered to the ground and I immediately pointed my gun at the second guy. His gun was already falling, as my intent was pretty clear.

I said, without looking at the other two white guys, "I suggest you take your balls and bats and go home, gentlemen. This game is over."

Everyone just stood there looking at me. No one moved. Not the vigilantes, not the diners. I took careful aim and shot at the first bat carrier. The bat exploded into splinters. The guy fell back but he wasn't hit. I'd made my point. The four vigilantes ran for their vehicles. I looked over at the diners. Two of them were off to the side, their hands hidden. I knew what was in them.

"Folks, I probably shouldn't have done that. What they're doing is legal. It just seemed wrong, somehow. Perhaps you'll forget what I look like. I'd appreciate that. Good night."

And, with that, I turned on my heel, stepped to the limousine and drove away. That had been a mistake. I know that no good deed goes unpunished.

Coming out of Barstow, we headed west on Interstate 15.

"Where am I going, Luis? We heading to LA? Canada? What have you decided?"

"To the Union Train station. Downtown LA. It is called LAX but it is not the airport. It is very busy and we should be able to get on a train without attracting any attention. We will take the Amtrak to San Diego and then the local to San Ysidro. That takes us to the border. We will walk across. That is our best way to get out of this mess."

"You figure that will work out okay, Luis?"

"I will be fine. I have a green card to show if I am picked up and the cops in California will not check to see that I registered. Sofía may have a problem if she is discovered on her own. If they do discover she has no papers it is likely they would send her back to Mexico."

"Papa," Sofía said quietly. "I have a plan. Don't get mad."

"Why would I be mad?"

"I wanted to come to LA. This was my plan all along for León and me. I'm going to marry Miguel. He is the real father of León. Aba doesn't know. That's a problem. A big problem. Only Miguel knows. I didn't tell you because it makes no difference to you. When I marry Miguel I can apply for this thing called advanced parole. It would let me go to Mexico and come back almost right away. I get some papers and permits and pay some lawyers and I come back to a green card.

"I'm gonna text Miguel that I'm in LA. We're getting back together today. We've been planning it. There's nothing you can do to stop it. I have a future with him. This is good for us, papa. Good for me and León. Just take me to Miguel. Please."

Mike Tyson famously once said, "Everybody has a plan until they get punched in the mouth." Luis had just been hammered.

"Sofía! This is crazy. You cannot be with those drug dealers. They are scum. Don't be loco."

"Papa, Miguel wants out. He has a house for me and León. He has money. He knows business. He's a good man. This is what I want. Just take us there, okay?"

"Does Miguel know we are coming?"

"He thought tomorrow, papa. I told him tomorrow because the truck was broken. Then, when we rented the van, I didn't have a chance to tell him. Not yet. I *have* to tell him. We can't show up if Aba is there."

"So, you are going to live with Miguel, get married and fill out forms for the lawyers? And what? Aba is just going to be the best man at your wedding?"

"Miguel is going to sort that out."

"How, Sofía? How is Miguel supposed to sort that out? Is he going to sell his half of the business to a guy who thinks he already owns it all? Is he going to ask for severance pay? I do not think so."

Luis went silent for a moment. The rage coming off him was palpable and intense.

"The plan is to kill Aba, is that not right, Sofía? Miguel is supposed to murder him. My daughter and her boyfriend kill a man and take his drug business. That's your brilliant plan, is it not?"

Sofía just hung her head.

Luis said, "I'm going to call Terry. He can call the LAPD. Let them sort it out."

"Papa, I want to save Miguel."

"Then call him and tell him to get out of his house. I suspect Aba knows, and if I think that, he probably does. Miguel has only minutes, if he is not dead already. And the only reason I do this is because Miguel is León's father."

Both of them got on their phones. Both of them had conversations that sounded like they'd gone as expected.

"What now, Luis?"

"I don't think anything changes. One drug dealer or another. No difference to me."

"When you go to Mexico you can come back to the US if you want, right, Luis? Or is your green card revoked because you didn't register?"

"I don't know, Charles, but honestly, I don't care right now. I only care about my family, even though I am so very ashamed of my daughter."

"Maybe you should stay in LA for a bit? Apply for that advanced parole thing?"

"I do not think so, Charles. Do not forget, we're associated with this vigilante situation. And Sofía may be associated with whatever goes down between Miguel and Aba. I really do not know how I will be treated in the short term, but I want to help my family. It is possible both Sofía and I could be arrested and then León would be in foster care. Anything is better than that. For his sake I want to get us all out of the country."

"Okay, I get it. But I'm going to make it easier for you, Luis. Don't argue with me on this. Just do it, okay? *I* killed the guy in Yucca. You were just a passenger in the back seat."

"Charles, that is crazy. Are you and Sofía smoking the same stuff? I am not letting you take that on. No way."

"Hear me out. Terry already knows I took out the first two vigilantes. What with the tinted windows, and you being in the back seat, no one knows where the shots came from, except maybe the dead guy, and he isn't talking. If the wounded guy had a glimpse of anything, it would've likely been me. Seriously, I can keep you out of it and we both know that self defense will likely carry the day, if it comes to that. Anyway, I intend to be in Canada by the time anyone accuses me of anything. Lucky for me, I guess, Arizona has the death penalty. Canada won't allow extradition. You admit to nothing. Deal?"

"I do not know, Charles. Maybe. If I let you do this and you ever need me, for anything, I am stepping up. I swear."

"I have no doubt, Luis."

CHAPTER TWENTY-FOUR — *Dale*

I saw the broken down vehicle a long way ahead. But cars break down all the time. Life is tough. I just kept driving. It was late. I was exhausted. *And* I was starving. Not to mention that Rufus would be, too.

The shoot out at the O.K. Corral had got the adrenaline flowing and that just made the whole thing worse. I was definitely feeling my age. Worse, fear of the four bubbas was dancing in my head. They were gonna be royally pissed. I'd humiliated them. They'd had to leave their shotguns in the parking lot. They'd hate me for that, too. I'd just made four enemies.

With all those thoughts whirling around in my mind I almost didn't see her. There had been just a bit of movement well ahead of the cones of light from my headlights. Usually, when I notice a slight movement, I see a coyote or rabbit or something. Not this time. The movement was different and, as a result, I glanced over to the side of the road as I drove by. I saw a face. It was a female face. She was hiding.

I stopped. Backed up most of the way. I got out and shouted back in the direction of where I knew she was crouching. "You don't have to hide from me. I'm not going to hurt you. If you need a ride, don't worry. I'm going to Picacho but, if you want, I'll go all the way to Tucson. My name is Dale. I drive this limousine for a living. If you're going to come, please let's go. I'm pretty tired and very hungry. I don't want to stand here waiting around like a fool."

The girl came up onto the side of the road about forty feet away. She looked like she was poised to run into the desert if I made a wrong move.

I looked her over. A teenager. Pretty shapely for a young girl. Long black hair. Jeans. Light jacket. No threat, but a target for some people. I turned and headed back to the open driver's door waving my arm in a gesture that suggested 'get in, let's get going'. She did.

Once inside she spoke assertively. It seemed she was trying to show me she wasn't an easy target. "My name is Ana. You said your name is Dale. Will you tell me your last name, mister?"

I smiled and pointed to my large ID and photo on the sun visor of the limo. This kid had a bit of spunk in her—that was good.

"Thanks for stopping for me. You're pretty old so I figured it was okay to take a ride. You seem nice, but you know, you never can tell."

Dale laughed. "It's okay. You're safe with me. Was that your car back there?"

"It's my parents' car. I don't drive. I don't know how and I don't have a license. But I took it because the vigilantes came and took my parents away. I was scared. But I think I broke the car. I couldn't get it to go very fast and then it stopped. Lots of red lights came on."

"Well, I can look at it tomorrow. Don't worry."

"I was really scared out there. I could only walk a few hundred yards before I saw a car coming and I had to hide. I'm afraid of the vigilantes or the cops finding me."

"You're safe now, Ana. Where are you headed?"

"Mexico."

"*Mexico*? All by yourself?"

"My parents told me to run. I have no other place to go. I'm an illegal now. They call me a Dreamer. I know it might not be safe but I have no choice."

"How old are you?"

"Fifteen."

"Ana, a fifteen year old girl cannot go to Mexico on her own. It's more than not safe, it's very dangerous. There are bad vigilantes all the way to the border and the cartels after that."

"I don't know what else to do."

"Don't you have some family or friends who can help?"

"I have friends in school. Some have families in trouble like mine so they can't help me. Some of my white friends' parents hate Mexicans, so I can't go to them. I have an aunt in Oregon. A place called Woodburn. It's near Portland. I could go there but it's a long way."

"But, what about your parents? When are they going to be released?"

"They probably won't be. My parents are illegals. We've been here for ten years but they will be deported. They know that."

"And so what are you supposed to do?"

"I guess I should go to the police. Go to jail. But I hid from the vigilantes and I'm glad I did. They hit my father and were rude to my mother. They tore her clothes. It was horrible."

"So, that's it? Some Mexican girl is supposed to survive on her own when her parents get deported? That can't be right."

"Señor, don't be angry. We're illegals. The police don't know I'm here. The police didn't separate us. The vigilantes did, when they took my parents. Our family took a chance to be here in this country, my mother says."

"Do you have any money?"

Ana reached into her small purse and pulled out twenty dollars. She tried to hand it to me.

"Ana, I don't want your money. I just wanted to know if you had any."

"I have this twenty dollars. You can have it."

"I told you, I don't want your money."

I pulled over at the local Walmart, between Eloy and Picacho. It looked like I was going to have to make my own dinner and I might as well feed Ana too.

"You hungry?"

She was. She came into the store with me. I walked over to the bakery section for bread and then got a dozen eggs. Ana carried the basket for me and followed behind. I started to head to the cashier.

"Is that it?"

"What do you want?"

"Let me shop."

"Fine. Knock yourself out."

Twenty minutes later, Ana wheeled a buggy half full of groceries back to the limousine. I was close to a hundred dollars lighter.

"Don't worry, Dale. I'll cook. You'll like it."

"I don't like Mexican food."

"I don't make Mexican food. I make Ana food. I promise you'll like it."

We headed home. An hour and a half later, Ana had proven her claim and we were both full and content. I offered Ana the bed but she said she wanted to sleep on the couch. There was no debate. She was asleep ten minutes later and I managed to take a shower before I was dead to the world.

Breakfast was magnificent. Even Rufus perked up.

"You're a good cook, Ana."

"Better than good, Dale. You know it."

I laughed. "You're right, you are *great*. Really great."

"I work after school with my mother at The Wild Horse Resort. I've learned a lot."

"You're too young. You're illegal. Your mother is an illegal. How is that possible?"

"My father has a fake green card. He got on as a groundskeeper at the golf course. He made friends in management. Then, when a woman left the kitchen staff, my mother went in and took her place. The human resources guy is Chicano and he made it happen. Last year, they made it happen again for me."

"You're all taking American jobs."

"Maybe. But we get paid less than minimum wage. No American will work for that."

"How do you know all this?"

"My dad says that as long as we work harder for less pay, Americans will make extra money and let us stay. He says, if I study hard, I can be an American someday and it will work that way for me too. He said America has always had slaves. Now it's our turn."

"Oh, man. Okay, well right now we have to get you out of here. This is what I think we should do. I take you to Phoenix and put you on a bus to Oregon. Don't worry; I'll pay for your ticket. I got a bonus yesterday. And you made dinner and breakfast so that makes us even. I've got a couple of calls to make and you need to call your aunt and tell her you're coming, okay?"

"I don't have her number. I don't have my phone."

"Well, we can look for the number while we drive. If we can't find it, we'll have to get someone from a church or something to meet you. Can you handle that?"

"Si, Dale. I'm not afraid anymore, not with you."

CHAPTER TWENTY-FIVE

Aba crossed the room to his computer. He brought up his bank account and typed in the password. The information was what he expected. His account was intact. If Miguel was planning something, he hadn't done it yet. But, one thing was clear; he had to change the password, and he'd better do it real soon. Problem was he didn't know how to change the password without Miguel's help. The bank account was set up with two parts to the password. They had to work together to make withdrawals. That kept the money safe, but now it was a problem for him. He was going to have to confront Miguel.

"I'm going to Miguel's. You guys ready?"

"You want us now?"

"Right now. You ready or not?"

The three heavies glanced at one another. One patted his holstered .357 Magnum and said, "Always ready."

The trio stood up and waited for Aba to take the lead. Aba opened his desk drawer and took out a pearl handled .45 and shoved it in the front of his pants. He grabbed the phone and dialed Miguel.

"Yo. Comin' over."

"Sure."

Miguel was close to panic. He had maybe two minutes before Aba was at his door. He grabbed his laptop, put it in a briefcase and thought for a second about a gun.

Another gun isn't going to help me, he decided. He knew there was a shotgun under the seat in the truck and a .45 in the glove compartment. He grabbed the briefcase and ran out the front door, not even bothering to see if it closed.

He was in his vehicle and leaving the curb when he saw the first of the Escalades coming down the street a block or so back. He accelerated hard and the Ford Raptor laid rubber and raced off. He didn't have to look. He knew they were coming for him.

His phone rang—Aba. "Yeah?"

"Why you drivin' away, man? Why you leave the house, eh, amigo? What you runnin' from, dawg?"

"I gotta get out, Aba. I was gonna tell you but there weren't no time. I'm out. That's it. Just out. You got no worries, man. You got everything, I just got a little. Should be no skin off you, man. I made you way more than I took. Just let me go easy, Aba."

There was a long silence. "You goin' alone, amigo?"

Miguel knew in that moment that he was going to be dead if Aba had his way. This wasn't going well.

"Me and Sofía, Aba. I'm the father. We didn't tell you 'cause you would've gone loco. We jus' tryin' to have a life, man."

"You gonna have a life, no question, bro. You and Sofía gonna have a life for sure. It just gonna be real short, mi amigo. Real, real short."

* * * * *

The thing about LA is that there are times when the traffic simply does not move. And, when that happens, if someone is chasing you and gets within a block of you, they can simply leave their car, run down the stalled lanes and get to you. And that was Aba's plan.

"You guys stay close. When Miguel's stopped, you two take that motherfucker down. Make sure we're slowed 'cause you no good to me runnin' down the freeway tryin' to get back in the car. Take your time. Pick the right place. Lil' Loco is gonna get us as close as possible. That fucker can drive so just don' let 'im get too far ahead o' ya."

Miguel *could* drive. He was fast and he had more than a few tricks up his sleeve. But right now the best tactic was to simply get some distance between him and Aba. The Ford Raptor helped. With a light aluminum body and 450 turbocharged horses it was a rocket ship. Much faster than Aba's vehicles, there wasn't enough room on LA's freeways to give the Raptor the playground it needed. It was also very nimble—he could put that to good use.

The Raptor has a unique hybrid traction system that combines the best of all-wheel drive with the best of four-wheel drive. Basically, that just means it will find grip where other vehicles might not. With Miguel driving, he would find grip where virtually no one could.

Traffic was getting heavier, slowing. Miguel weaved towards the outside shoulder lane. There was no exit ramp, but he knew that. He put his foot to the floor and raced down the shoulder as far as he could before it disappeared as the highway became an overhead above another freeway. He squeezed into the slow-moving traffic just before he would have been stopped at the bottleneck.

Lil' Loco had followed closely, but it took him longer to get the Escalade to the shoulder lane and that meant they were squeezed by the narrowing highway before he and Aba had covered the same distance. Miguel had picked up maybe one hundred yards with that simple maneuver, as traffic ground to a halt.

Miguel had gained some distance but, if traffic stopped, the shooters could be at his window in seconds. He needed to put more distance between them.

He was on the 110, heading towards the Harborway overpass and the 9th Street exit. He was in the middle lane and crossed to the outer lane to gain access to the exit. That maneuver cost him some ground. Aba was just a few hundred feet behind now and had remained in the far right lane. He hadn't had to move over or slow down to take the exit.

Miguel dove down the ramp to the congestion that was on James Wood Avenue, heading to the intersection at Figueroa. He saw an opening and quickly crossed three lanes of heavy traffic to exit on Cottage, heading south. That was a very lucky move and not one Aba could possibly replicate. At the end of Cottage he thought he might have lost them. His last sighting was them trying to exit the ramp. He couldn't imagine they'd make the Cottage jump.

He was wrong. As they approached the congestion on James Wood, Aba had grabbed one of the shotguns and started shooting at cars approaching from the right. The blasts were loud enough to be heard by every vehicle. The ones that were hit got the message fast and slammed to a halt. Aba's two SUVs sprinted across to Cottage and down it, just in time to see Miguel turn right again on Georgia.

"Makes no sense, homie. He headin' back to James Wood. We got it totally jammed there. What he thinkin'?"

Miguel hadn't thought it would be clear but the shooting had made it more of a jam than he'd expected. He'd known that getting through the jam was not going to be easy, but now it looked impossible. He was going to have to be extremely aggressive. Slow-moving commuters can stop more easily than when the traffic is moving steadily. He was just going to have to muscle through.

By the time he got to the intersection that plan needed some modification. Seemed something had caused complete gridlock and he could see people getting out of their cars. Worse, he saw in his rearview mirror the first of Aba's vehicles turning onto Georgia.

He lurched forward. Pushing into the first lane was the hardest part. Seems traffic was trying to merge into the north lane to get around whatever had caused those fuckers to get out of their cars. The first lane was gridlocked. The little luck he had was in the form of the small Miata two-seater right in front of him.

He leaned out the window and yelled, "Drive onto the sidewalk or I gonna drive over yo' ass!"

The driver was an attractive older woman. She glanced at him and then simply looked away. He pushed the Raptor against the back fender of her car, and inched forward. Then he backed up slightly and waved the piece from the glove compartment. That got her attention. She took the opportunity to move onto the sidewalk.

By then, Aba was close enough to release his boys. Miguel could see two guys getting out of the first vehicle. The second one had a door open and a third guy was getting out. This was getting too close.

Miguel now occupied the Miata lane and a Honda CRV, with what looked like a stubby little kayak on top, was in the middle lane. He pointed the .45 at the driver of the CRV. The guy just looked at Miguel and held his hands in a helpless gesture to indicate he could not move. Miguel had to make a decision. He drove his front bumper against the side of the Honda and put his foot to the floor.

The CRV started to move sideways into the third lane which was still moving slowly. The guy in the third lane, who would have been next to move up beside the CRV, was aware that it was being pushed sideways across his lane. That was enough to make him stop and make the right decision to give up his turn to move forward.

By now Miguel was moving but he wasn't moving fast enough. He switched to 4x4 and felt the big truck gain some traction. He and the CRV continued up the entrance ramp, but not much quicker than Aba's guys could run. It was getting way too close again.

Miguel stopped halfway up the ramp. He had to back up a bit to clear the CRV out of his way. Logic would suggest that he drive around the front of the CRV and head up the rest of the way. Miguel was smarter than that.

He knew the ramp only led to more congestion so he took another path instead. That path led him up the slope that separated the bottom of the ramp from the freeway. It would put him only a few feet away from the Exit 9 ramp he'd used less than ten minutes before. It was a gamble to take that exit. Aba was still down there. Miguel knew, though, that the traffic there was at a standstill. If he could loop around fast enough, he could take Exit 9 to get to Figueroa while Aba and his guys were still trapped in traffic. Even better, if he drove slowly, they might not see him do the loop.

LA freeways are generally pretty ugly but the city does what it can to make them more attractive when possible. The entrance ramp, just after Exit 9, that makes the transition from the lower James Wood level to the higher Interstate 110 level, is a case in point. The sides of it are clad in poured concrete with small boulders set every so often to break the visual monotony. Aesthetically it leaves a lot to be desired. But, for the Raptor's 4x4 grip, coupled with over 500 foot pounds of torque, it was a junior level climbing wall.

Miguel crested the top of the incline, turned left into the face of traffic and drove the wrong way down the shoulder to make the Exit 9 off-ramp. As he descended down to the same street he'd just scrambled away from, he kept the truck to the left of the ramp, to minimize the chance of being noticed. Unfortunately, that meant he couldn't see Aba either. But he *could* see that traffic was grid-locked back up James Wood. Some people were helping the guy in the CRV, leaving their cars in the road, which just added to the confusion. In fact, the jam was so bad that Miguel now feared that he would be seen simply because his was one of the only vehicles moving out ahead of all the chaos.

He got to Figueroa and turned left. If Aba had seen him there was no way they could extricate themselves from the mess they were in except to back down Georgia and go from there. By the time they did that, he'd be gone.

CHAPTER TWENTY-SIX

"Agent Henry? Rodriguez. Car chase on Interstate 110 heading into town. Shots fired. Traffic is a mess. Cameras suggest it was two Escalades chasing down a Ford Raptor. They exited at 9th Street. We think it was Miguel's truck. He got away."

"Where to?"

"Not sure. If it's him in the Ford Raptor, he's pretty fast. His route was, well, creative to say the least. So far, we think he's heading up Figueroa but we haven't picked him out yet. The cameras and the computers are scanning but nothing yet."

"Who do you think is chasing him?"

"Most likely Aba and his crew. They were caught in the same jam but backed up and got out. Right now, we have them down town heading north on Figueroa as well. But they're going slow. Hunting, I guess."

"LAPD on this?"

"Yes and no. We got uniforms on the ground taking statements and the preliminaries show that we may have something on Miguel. People notice a Raptor. But someone else fired off a shotgun and that makes a bit of an impression, too."

"So, no officers following Aba?"

"Not yet—I've sent in a request. But Aba has presumably done nothing yet. He's just looking."

"Never mind, my team's on the way. They got left in the dust back at Compton but knew enough to stay on the freeway. They're probably closer to headquarters than we are. I'll leave them there to see if the cameras find Miguel. If they do, we have a chance of getting to him before Aba does."

"Sir, is your primary target now Miguel or still the fugitives from Arizona?"

"Good point. It has to be the fugitives, but let's hope they're going to meet up with Miguel. He's our bait. Find that truck."

* * * * *

Miguel's phone rang—Sofía. "Where are you?"

"Safe for now. Downtown. Aba an' his guys are after me. Can you pick me up?"

"Yeah. Sure. Where?"

"Can you get to Loyola Marymount? Go to the student entrance at the University Hall parking garage. I'll wait for you there.

"Nancy's driving. We could miss a turn. Give us an hour, okay?"

"Okay, you don' have to hurry. I can hang out there with no problem. I'll be waiting. What you drivin'?"

* * * * *

Aba was impressed with Miguel's driving ability. And he was aware that Miguel knew the area well, especially around Loyola Marymount—Miguel had gone to university there. That didn't mean he was going to head there but it did mean he would know how to get out of the city from there. But get out to where? Where would he go? And wasn't Miguel planning on meeting up with Sofía? If they were meeting up, where would they do that?

"Head over to Loyola Marymount. I got a hunch."

CHAPTER TWENTY-SEVEN — *Dale*

"Beth, it's Dale, the limo driver. Remember me?"

"Sure, Dale. Not all limo drivers are tall and handsome."

Dale laughed. "Thanks, for that, Beth, but I can't flirt right now. Gotta talk to Terry. Is he in?"

"I'll put you through."

"Terry, it's Dale. The limo driver."

"I know who you are, Dale. See you and your limo all the time out at the range. What's up?"

"Well, there was a shooting last night at some Mexican restaurant. Did you hear about it?"

"Nope. No reports of shots fired. That's weird. Probably just some idiot, or maybe a gang thing. Why?"

"It was me. I shot twice. Once in the air, once at a baseball bat."

"You'd better start explaining."

I told Terry what had happened and he agreed immediately that getting into the middle of it had been pretty dumb.

"I can guess your politics, Dale. Slightly right of Attila the Hun. I would've half expected you to side with the bats."

"Well then, you'd be wrong now, wouldn't you, Terry. I believe in law and order. That's why I'm calling you. And I don't believe in what they were doing, or even what I did. We were all vigilantes. Problem is they were made legal by the government. I wasn't."

"Well, for what it's worth, the crackdown has created a shit storm of trouble. We got innocent people being hurt, jailed and families arrested. It's crazy. I believe in law and order, too, but I believe in laws that have been well thought through and implemented properly. This was just a presidential order written in a fucking tweet. We got nothing but trouble on this one."

"Yeah, well, I may have added to it."

"Don't worry. No reports were made. I don't have to follow up. But you better keep an eye out for the four assholes you messed up. They may hold a grudge."

"Okay, but I've done more than just that, Terry." I told him about shaking down passengers for the bounty. "It seemed like the right thing to do at the time. They *were* lawbreakers, after all. And I liked the easy money at first. But now, after last night, I'm not so sure. Now, it feels like I'm part of something that's hurting innocent people. I don't feel good about that."

"Dale, we haven't had a call about that, either. Maybe you should check with your company. They may have had complaints. Maybe you can right that wrong on your own."

"Okay. And there is one more thing, Terry."

"Oh, this is just great. You're the gift that keeps on giving."

"I picked up a young Mexican girl on the highway last night. Her name's Ana. She's fifteen. Some vigilantes took her parents. She said it got rough. She hid from the vigilantes and then ran. I found her."

"What are you going to do with her?"

"I'm asking you."

"Well, whatever you do, don't turn her in. Both Eloy and Florence are at double capacity. They even have young kids sharing the yard with hardened criminals. This whole thing is going to get much worse before it gets better. You could try one of the Mexican churches, but I know they're pretty overwhelmed. Can't you let her stay at your place for a while?"

"Christ, Terry, I'm an old white male. You wanna know how long it would take before you had to come and arrest me if some feminazi found out I even talked to her? Are you out of your mind?"

"You're right. You gotta get her somewhere. Push comes to shove, drop her here and we'll put her in juvenile detention. It's full to bursting, too, but it's a hell of a lot better than Eloy or Florence. If you have to drop her, make sure it's a church or here."

"I can put her on a bus to Oregon. She's got family there."

"That might be best, but make sure she gets on the bus in California. We've had reports of vigilantes setting up all along the state line. They've stopped more than a few buses before they got over."

"That doesn't leave me much choice, does it?"

"I told you; drop her with us if you have to. I understand."

"Thanks, Terry." Dale hung up.

"You *shot* someone last night?"

"No, no, Ana. I shot a guy's baseball bat. He was threatening people. I told him to put his bat down. He wouldn't. So I shot it."

"Was he mad?"

"Not at the time. But by now he likely is and I'm not happy about that."

"But wasn't it the right thing to do?"

"I dunno, Ana. Does anyone know what the right thing is anymore?"

I called into work and told them I needed the day off. I mentioned I was taking the limo. Family emergency. Then I called Fred at the auto repair in town and asked him to tow Ana's car in and have a look at it.

"I'm driving you to California, Ana. This is crazy. I don't even like Mexicans and here I am driving you in a limousine to California and paying for it myself. This is really nuts."

Ana smiled. "I can make it worth your while, Dale."

"*What?*" I was shocked at the seduction I heard in her voice. "*What are you saying?*"

Ana laughed and said, "If it's not safe to take me to the bus station in Phoenix, it's not safe for some of the people there to get on a bus. Let's make the trip worthwhile and take some others. It won't cost you extra and we can help more people."

I just looked at her for a minute and burst out laughing. "Okay, why not? And you, Ana, have a naughty streak." We both laughed.

"I think we have to make room for one more, Dale." Ana had gone into the bus station, found a woman with four kids, explained the situation and, within a minute, the limousine was full of chattering Mexicans. I wasn't happy.

"No more. This was a stupid idea in the first place. Can't you make them shut up?"

"Señor, we are grateful for your help. I will tell my children to be quiet. You will have no problem with us."

"Oh. You speak English? Good. I'm sorry I was rude. It's just that this is so crazy."

"It is not you, señor. It is not even the Americans. It is your president, señor. He has hate in his heart."

Dale didn't answer her. To Ana he said, "No more people, we have a full car."

"This guy needs to come." Ana pushed a slim, well-dressed middle-aged man into the front seat. Dale took one look and said, "No way! No A-rabs, Ana. No A-rab terrorist sons of bitches . . . get this guy out!"

"Please, sir, I'm not an A-rab son of a bitch. I'm a Persian from Iran. I'm *not* an Arab. Allow me to introduce myself. I'm Fahdzi Tehrani. I'm a doctor, not a terrorist."

"I don't care what the hell kind of an A-rab you are, Abdulla, I'm not giving you a ride. Get out."

"Of course, sir. My apologies. I'll leave."

"You stay where you are, Fahdzi," Ana said. "Dale, he has all his papers and yet he's been thrown into Eloy three times already. He can't get out of Arizona fast enough. Every time he shows his face, he's grabbed by vigilantes. You *can't* kick him out. He has less of a chance out there than I do."

I put my head in my hands. What the hell difference did it make at this point? "Okay. Sit there. Shut up. I don't like fucking A-rabs. Not one bit. So, take the ride and just shut the hell up, okay?"

"Yes, sir," Fahdzi said, turning to look forward and adopting a stern countenance to illustrate his feelings, "but, for the record, I don't like fucking A-rabs either."

I could hardly contain myself. That was pretty funny. But I kept my amusement to myself and sighed, "Jesus!"

The Greyhound station was just off the I-10. The stop hadn't taken fifteen minutes. We were back on the road and heading west soon after.

"What was Eloy like?"

Fahdzi looked over at me. I was genuinely curious. I had tried to ask without tone in my voice. It seems he felt it was safe to answer truthfully. "The first time was very expedient. The first official to see me reviewed my papers and released me. I spent more time in the truck with the vigilantes than I spent in Eloy. The officials were efficient and they apologized. No bribes were required. They just let me go."

"The second time?"

"Much the same, but it took much longer because there were so many more people lined up. After six hours I was seen, my papers examined and I was let go. They were apologetic also. However, it was the third time that I found most alarming."

"What happened?"

"It was the evening after I was released for the second time. I was walking across the parking lot of my hotel. Vigilantes apprehended me and took me to Eloy once again. There was no room there so I was dispatched to Florence. I was there for many hours, sharing one small cell with three others. Some of my fellow detainees were rather terrifying. It was exceptionally hot and everyone was very much on edge. The guards were nasty and hit inmates with their sticks for no reason. I perceived it to be a very dangerous situation. When I got out, I vowed to leave Arizona immediately. Some of the others I spoke to informed me that going to the airport was guaranteed to get me apprehended yet again. I had hoped the bus station would be the solution. But if it wasn't for you, I'd be back in Eloy again."

"How do you know that?"

"Just before Ana came in, I noticed that a rather rough looking fellow had entered the waiting room and was counting people. He seemed to be looking only at people with dark skin. His gaze lingered on me. I knew I had been included in his count."

"Why did Ana choose you?"

"She didn't. I heard her speaking with the family next to me. I asked her to consider me. I told her why. She just told me to follow her."

"So, Ana, you don't just save Mexicans, it seems. You're an equal-opportunity heroine, I guess."

"Dale, we're all the same. My parents said we are. I feel we're all the same, don't you?"

"Not lately, Ana. Not lately."

"This isn't the America I expected, Dale," Fahdzi commented. "Far more poor people than I expected. And so much violence."

"Well, this isn't really America, Fhadzi. This is something new. I don't know what it is but it isn't America. Not like I know it. We don't allow vigilantism in my America. We're law abiding people."

"But America has always been violent. You're always at war with somebody. Americans have more guns than people. This is a dangerous country, especially for a foreigner."

"That might be true for you. But you knew that. You came anyway. So, what's the surprise? What did you expect?"

"I don't know. Less poverty, certainly. That's why I'm asking. I expected opportunity. I expected to be welcomed. Was I wrong? What's happening? Is the American dream true or not?"

"Hah! The American Dream has never been true, Fhadzi. Not for everyone, anyway. They say only one percent gets that dream. I think it's a bit higher but the American dream is not everyone's dream, anyway. Being filthy rich and a celebrity is not everyone's goal. Most Americans just want to live a long and healthy life in peace and have some fun doing it. That's all I ever wanted."

"What happened, Dale? Why couldn't you have your dream?"

"I dunno. School trained me for nothing except football. The army trained me for shooting. That's not really a marketable skill. And Joanne and I couldn't have kids. She got ill. That was a tough time. Then she died. We were always in debt. I really don't know, Fhadzi. I really don't. I worked hard. Just always in debt. I really don't know why my life turned out like it did."

"Do you blame Mexicans, Dale?"

"No. Of course not. Not really. Not even A-rabs. They don't make it any easier, though. No Mexican does my yard. No Mexican cleans my house. They just gather in communities and eat and have kids and play horrible fucking music too loud. Plus, the young guys are punks. Some of them, anyway. They should all go into the army for five years. Give something back."

"Be like you?"

"Hah! That's funny Fhadzi. No, no one should be like me."

"Nancy, stay on Highway 10 'til you can switch to 101 West," Sofía instructed. "Okay, now go for a bit and take the 110 South. The Loyola Marymount exit comes up pretty quick. It's the 8th Street exit but it says Loyola Marymount on the sign as well. You're doin' good. We don't have to go too fast."

Nancy took the Loyola Marymount exit, followed 8th Street to Union, turned left and then left again on Olympic. The student parking garage came into view on our left.

"That's it. Pull in here. You can go right to the student entrance. Miguel should show up. If he doesn't, turn around and get us faced in the opposite direction, put on your signal lights and get in the passenger seat. Miguel knows the city backwards. He should drive."

"Sofía, I don't feel comfortable having Miguel drive."

"Okay, your call. But, if you don't let him drive, at least go where he says. He knows the city better than Google. Seriously."

"Fine."

Nancy turned on Albany. She didn't notice the Escalade parked three spots down from the corner. Aba and his guys didn't pay much attention to the van, either. They were looking for a Raptor.

She pulled up to the parkade entrance. There was a parking spot across the street, a few spaces up. After stopping to see if there was anyone waiting, she slowly crept forward to half occupy the parking spot. If a cop came she could park. Otherwise, she was off the road and not bringing too much attention to herself. I was beside her. Luis, Sofía and León were in the back seat. No one spoke.

* * * * *

Miguel was relieved. He'd been standing in the shadows and was getting anxious. When the van pulled up, he walked out carrying the briefcase. The pistol was in his other hand. That might have been a mistake.

"Aba, some dude up there carryin' . . . he's walkin'. . . "

Aba looked out, "It's Miguel. Call the others. Tell 'em to block the other end of the street. Let's go."

The big Escalade pulling out abruptly caught Miguel's attention. He knew instantly he'd been spotted. As he ran to the van he saw another vehicle farther up pull out across the street. They had him blocked in. No sense getting Sofía and the baby hurt. He ran to the driver's side and said, "Get out of here. They're at both ends of the street. They want me, not you. Take the case and go!"

Nancy yelled, "Get in! C'mon!"

Sofía opened the sliding back door and Miguel jumped in. Miguel shouted "Go! There's an alley!

Nancy took off and turned at the alley, blasted down to Blaine and turned right. There was a UPS van directly ahead of us.

"Go around," said Miguel.

The light was with us at Olympia with two more big brown UPS trucks blocking the way, one turning left and the other turning right.

Nancy chose to go between them as they both turned in two different directions. There didn't appear to be enough room as she closed in, but she accelerated and hit the gap with basically nothing to spare.

Sofía shrieked, "Ay Dios mio!"

"Turn right at the alley at the far end of the next building," Miguel shouted.

There was no alley visible. But Nancy turned anyway. An impossibly narrow lane appeared. She made the turn, drifted around the corner, and accelerated hard.

"Quick left and then right at the next street."

That zigzag, executed at speed, put us on West 10th Place but, more critically, it took us out of view of our pursuers. The passengers in the back were crushed together so they weren't being flung around too much. I was holding on for dear life.

"Turn left on Valencia. Then left again on 11th. Don't stop. Not for lights. Not for anything. Take the freeway entrance whether you have the light or not. Don't worry. No cars coming from the right. Blaine is one way."

Nancy didn't try to process what Miguel was saying. She simply found a path and shot through as fast as she could. She took the turns and, at 11th, she wasn't sure if there was a stop sign or what. Made no difference, she was going anyway.

At Blaine the traffic was stopped and waiting for through-flow traffic accessing the freeway on-ramp. Some cars turned right from Blaine and were coming straight at her on 11th. She was driving against the flow and taking what road she needed. At the light she turned right, merged with traffic, and headed up the ramp. By the time they hit the freeway, Nancy had passed a dozen more cars and was looking for more space to fill.

"Slow down. You did good. We got through at least three bottlenecks, especially at Blaine and the on-ramp. Gutsy moves. They're not behind us. I'm Miguel."

"Gutsy? Didn't you tell me not to stop?"

"Yeah, I just didn't think you'd take me literally. That was some driving, especially for an abuela."

"Nice to meet, you Miguel," Nancy said. "You're turning out to be such a charmer."

CHAPTER THIRTY — *Charlie*

"Oh, fuck!" Miguel had seen something.

"What now?" I asked.

"Aba's in front of us. They must have given up the chase and headed for the freeway, going straight down Blaine. We did a loop for nothing. We're just a dozen cars back. Fuck!"

"Calm down," I said. "Maybe this is good. It's unlikely they've seen us. Just drop back a bit farther, Nance. This just might work out all right."

"Okay," said Miguel, sounding a little more composed. "Stay in the same lane as he's in. Keep close to the car in front of you. If you give up space between cars, trust me, an Angelino will fill it. We can drop back, but we have to stay in the same lane. Did you see the second car?"

"No. I don't know what it is."

"It's a black Escalade, also. Nothing to distinguish it except blacked out windows."

Nancy partially pulled out into the fast lane to get a better view of the middle lane they were traveling in. She didn't know cars well but she knew our friend Kerry drove an Escalade and there was an SUV, fitting that image, a few cars ahead of Aba.

She let a delivery truck in ahead of us. It blocked our view but no one ahead of us would see us even if they did look back.

"Where are we headed?" I asked.

"Aba's likely going back to his crib. The farther south we go, the more likely I am to be recognized, so I have to stay in the back. He has people all over LA so nowhere is safe, really, 'cept maybe Beverley Hills."

"Why Beverley Hills?"

"Those rich people got their own suppliers and they also got lots of private security around. A Bentley would be a better ride, but a soccer mom van driven by a white grandma is better than nothing."

"Thanks for that, Miguel. You *are* a sweetie," Nancy said as she took the next exit, swung through a few side streets according to his directions and, once again, we were headed north.

We left the Caravan at the north side of Beverley Gardens on Parkway. The six of us walked down Cannon, crossed Santa Monica and settled in at a Chipotle Mexican Grill. We were all famished. Everything tasted good. Twenty minutes later, we were full and happy. Life was good again.

Over lunch Miguel dropped most of his attitude. His speech patterns had changed. What's going on, Miguel? I finally asked.

"It's time to tell you all something. My cover is blown anyway, 'cause I can't go back."

"Your cover?" Sofía looked stunned.

"I've been working undercover for three years. I'm a cop. We've got enough on Aba to send him back to prison for a long time. We were hoping for a bit more, but circumstances overtook us. I'm out now. I just have to call in and get the guys to come and pick me up. They'll want to talk to all of you, too."

Sofía sat speechless for a moment. "You're a cop?"

"Yeah. Sorry. I hope you're not disappointed. I don't have the money you think I have. I'm not the man you think I am. Only two things you know about me are true. I love you. And I love León."

Sofía looked at Miguel as if he was a stranger. She looked at León and Luis. As her face turned pale, I saw tears pouring down her cheeks. She was shaking and weeping and coming apart. She needed someone.

Both Luis and Miguel moved to comfort her. They stopped and looked at each other. Luis stayed back and gestured to Miguel. Miguel enveloped Sofía and León in his arms.

"So, Luis, it turns out Sofía's instincts about Miguel were right."

"Yes, maybe, Charles. At some level. I hope so, anyway. But she fell in love with a drug dealer and is now in the arms of the police. Extremely ironic, Charles. But I am pleased. Miguel is probably going to be all right, after all. I hope he will make a good father. Being a police officer will likely help Sofía get a green card and, perhaps, keep her straight. I might just stick around and help them with the garden."

"What garden?"

"The one attached to the house I help them buy."

I hesitated to intrude on the family situation, but I had to. "Miguel, there's something you should know." I then explained Nancy and my predicament to him and, of course, he suggested we turn ourselves in.

"And what will happen to us then, Miguel?"

"Well, they'll review your story and, if it checks out, they'll release you. Probably you'll just have to leave the country."

"And, if we don't come in voluntarily, will you arrest us?"

"I'm sorry, Charlie. I have no choice."

"I understand, Miguel. You have your job to do. And I apologize for any inconvenience we might cause you."

"What do you mean?"

I looked at Nancy. We both stood up with our packs in hand and walked away from the table towards the door.

Miguel started to get out of his chair when he felt a hand, with a very solid grip on his shoulder, pushing him back into his seat. "Stay where you are, chico," said Luis. He left no room for disagreement.

Interstate 10 crosses the Arizona-California state line about ten or so miles west of Quartzite, Arizona. This time of year Quartzite is packed with wintering RVers. The kids desperately needed a pee break and getting something to eat at the same time would be good. I figured that if we got there, without running into any vigilante road blocks, we were likely home free and safe to have a quick stop.

My wife and I used to camp at Quartzite in the old days. It wasn't too far to drive in our old camper and we stayed for free on land that belongs to the Bureau of Land Management. There are always thousands of recreational vehicles there and people come from all over the world. Folks come from every walk of life. RVers are pretty independent and they're tolerant of other RVers, no matter who they are. That means Canadians and Americans alongside Mexicans and African-Americans. I even met a guy from Africa there once. No vigilantes, for sure. The bumper sticker I had says it all— "If you don't like me, move. If you won't move, I will."

But we weren't there yet. As we approached the overpass at Ramsey Road I noticed a guy on it and a few vehicles parked underneath on the side of the freeway. It didn't look like a welcoming party. I sped up to seventy-five and told Fahdzi to sit way back in the seat while I pushed my white face farther forward.

As we passed under the overpass, I noticed several tough looking uglies sitting in the shade smoking. They obviously had the chase vehicles and the guy on the bridge was the lookout. Still, it didn't make much sense to me. By the time the lookout got a good view of who was coming, the target vehicle would have passed at speed and it would take the trucks some time to catch up.

That's when I saw how the plan worked. Up ahead, just before the junction of I-10 with 60 and the exit that leads to Brenda, was a big eighteen-wheeler ready to pull out and block the highway. As I passed I saw another chase vehicle beside it. Lucky we were in the limo—obviously they didn't think we were who they were looking for. We'd just blown by a highway trap—no doubt an effective one. Vehicles could be stopped, checked and then driven out along 60 into Brenda without causing much of a hiccup in traffic flow. It was very efficient. I wondered how many people had been pulled over. I wondered if all this was what the government intended with their new laws. It reminded me, somehow, of Vietnam. Politics. What the hell was really going on?

The Aguilando family consisted of Maria, her eldest, Tomas, maybe twelve, and three little girls, Leticia, Yolanda and Salma, each a few years apart. I guessed Salma to be five but, to me, Maria didn't even look old enough to have kids—I guess I can't really tell anymore. They had been quiet as mice since my outburst a couple of hours ago.

"Can I ask where your husband is, Maria?"

"Dead. He was killed two years ago."

"Oh, I'm very sorry. What happened?"

"Carlos was a journalist, señor. They kill journalists in Mexico."

"Who does?"

"The cartels, mostly. But corrupt cops, politicians and bureaucrats, also. If you write a story that offends people in power, they kill you. Investigative journalism is all but dead in Mexico. And that's because so many journalists have been killed. Many who are left do not report everything because of the threat of death."

"That's terrible. Is that why you're in Arizona?"

"Yes. Carlos sent us here to be safe."

"And now the vigilantes?"

"Si, señor. Maybe. Maybe the cartels just used the excuse of the vigilantes."

"What do you mean?"

"It's not enough to kill the journalist, señor. Often family members are killed too. It sends a message. When we saw the vigilantes, we could not be sure who they were. We just had to run. We have green cards. But cards won't protect us from either group."

"So, you don't feel safe anywhere?"

"No, señor. And maybe you shouldn't either."

I was shocked. Reporters killed for reporting the news? That would never happen in the good old US of A. No wonder we needed a wall. And why shouldn't I feel safe? Of course I was safe in my own country. As long as I obeyed the law nothing would ever happen to me. The US isn't some third-world two-bit country where people act outside the law.

"You guys want something to drink or eat? Maybe some ice cream? I can stop in Quartzite. I think it'll be safe there."

"Si, señor. Please. I have money. I will pay."

I didn't respond. It seemed right that she pay and yet, for some reason, I thought *I* should.

"It's okay, Maria. You can let him pay. He's atoning for past sins, aren't you, Dale?"

"I am *not*, Ana. You stop that. This is *not* atonement. This is simply the fact that no good deed goes unpunished. My good deed stopping for *you* is being punished."

"Then you are in for a lot more trouble, señor," said Maria. "You picked us up, too."

"I agree with Ana and Maria, Dale. You also rescued an A-rab. It doesn't get any worse than that."

Everyone, including me, laughed out loud.

Quartzite, in full swing, had temporary tents and awnings for the services that catered to the overflowing area of RVs. Signage was poor, but traffic slowed to a crawl, and we soon found what we were looking for. I pulled over at what looked like a covered market and everyone spilled out. I stretched, looked around and yelled at everyone, "Hey! Back at the car in fifteen minutes. Don't make me wait."

Fahdzi waved an arm to indicate that I'd been heard and I watched them, looking like one big happy family, disappear into the first large tent. I wandered over to another one, closer to the car, and bought a coke. I smelled barbecue and walked a couple of tents over and picked up a burger.

I walked back to the car and enjoyed my meal. And mentally noted when fifteen minutes had passed. Kids were impossible so they were likely the cause of any delay. I sat for another few minutes and then had a horrible feeling. I got out of the car and half ran to the big tent.

There was a crowd about halfway down the main aisle of the tent and, in the middle of it, was Fahdzi. There were two state troopers checking his papers. Ana, Maria and the kids were all by his side.

"Officers, I'm Dale Barnes. Mr. Tehrani is my passenger. I'm with Ideal Limo Service in Phoenix. Is there a problem?"

"You driving Ali-Baba and this group around, bud? Can I see some ID?"

I showed him my operator's license and a few other pieces of ID. By now, my adrenaline was up and I was spoiling for a fight. I asked, with just a little sarcasm, "Officer, would you like to see my passport? I also have an Army Rangers' tattoo on my ass."

The bastard looked me up and down, thought better of saying anything and said to his partner, "They're legit. Let's go."

"You really got a Ranger's tattoo on your ass, Dale?"

Ana had a way of making me laugh. I stood there smiling while everyone else finished up what they'd been doing when they were interrupted by the troopers. None of the vendors charged my passengers for anything. Some apologies were even offered. I think I was the only one who paid for my lunch that day. Seemed fitting, somehow. Maybe I *was* atoning . . .

We got back on the freeway and headed west. I was thinking I might be able to discharge my responsibility for my passengers in Palm Springs. That would be more than fair. No one could expect more. They had some money for tickets. Palm Springs had buses. We could all shake hands and go our separate ways.

"Thank you, Dale, for coming to my rescue. The police officers didn't seem happy with my responses to their questions."

"Oh, they were just doing their job, Fahdzi. An A-rab with a bunch of Mexicans in Quartzite, of all places, would catch anyone's attention. They were just checking you out."

"True, Dale. I don't blame them. I just don't understand why they don't listen when I speak to them. They wouldn't listen when Maria spoke, either. They only listened when you spoke."

"Yeah. Well, police have selective hearing, *Ali-Baba*. You gotta use the right words."

Fahdzi looked thoughtful for a bit and said, "Yes. It's like that in my country, also."

"There are no right words to say to the policía in Mexico," Maria said. "You just bow your head and do as they say. Sometimes, you can give them money and they will go away. But you do not speak. If you speak, they hit you. Sometimes in America, too."

Dale's sense of law and order was different than that. His way, everyone obeyed the law and, if they didn't, the police could, and should, arrest them. But there was no need for harassment. There was no need to hit women and children. When did the police become less like a service to the community and more like a gang?

"Do you know what you're going to do in California, Maria?"

"I don't know, señor. We have green cards and California is safer than Arizona but I had a job in Arizona. I will have to get another job there. Carlos used to send us money before . . . so it's harder now. We can live with my sister. We're close. She's a good sister, but with four kids it's not fair to stay a long time, so I want to get my own place as soon as I can. I'm worried about getting a job and a place again."

"You're not afraid, are you?"

"Yes, I'm afraid. I'm afraid all the time. I've been afraid for so long it feels normal. I know nothing else now. These are bad times. 'Making America Great Again' is making it worse for us."

"You'll be fine once we get to California."

"Maybe, señor. But that's easy to say when you're white."

I thought about what Maria had just said. She believed what she said. But America is the home of the free, right? One country under God. Whatever color we are, we all bleed the same red blood of patriots.

I turned on the radio without thinking. The car had been relatively quiet. I guessed that everyone sensed that Palm Springs would be where we would part. It was a bit awkward. I guess I needed something to distract me.

"The program I instituted last Monday by order, I signed an order, is making America great again. Yuge success. Yuge. Even the fake media is reporting how great this is. And the great policemen and women in Arizona are doing America's work. America's work. Big success. Criminals are running for the border. People are saying they're running. Arizona is working for the American people."

"What the hell is he going on about? It's bloody chaos in Arizona. What kind of idiot would take credit for such a complete screw-up?"

"Your president doesn't tell the truth, Dale. Everyone knows that."

"Well, the media never tells the truth either. That's for sure."

"Maybe they all lie."

"Damn right. But Trump's different. He tells it like he sees it. If he thinks things are going well and they're not, then the blame is on his staff. Or maybe the media. Trump is straight."

Fahdzi and Maria fell silent.

"C'mon! He's not politically correct, and he doesn't always know what he's doing, but he tells it like it is. He's mad that America isn't as great as it was and he's trying to fix that. Isn't that clear to you guys?"

"By arresting my family, Dale? By hiring vigilantes? Will that make America great again? If you get rid of the Mexicans, will America be great again?"

"Of course not, Ana. You and Maria, and even Fahdzi here, are no threat. You probably work hard. Good for the country and all that. But what about the rapists and the drug dealers, eh? What about the terrorists, eh? Those people have to be sent away. That only makes sense."

"If you say so, Dale. But the only people I know who are running away are good people. Maybe the president is right. Maybe the drug dealers are running too. Maybe we are wrong to run. Maybe they will let my parents out of jail and we can go home again. Maybe those state troopers will take care of us."

"I told you, Ana, they were just doing their job."

"I know. Their job is to find Mexicans who rape, right? And sell drugs. And Muslims who are terrorists, right?"

Everyone fell silent. I turned the radio off. That newscast had created a bad feeling in the car. It was strange how ugly everything felt all of a sudden. How did one presidential statement make the atmosphere in the car feel so different? Now I *wanted* to get rid of them in Palm Springs. I accelerated. We'd be there in a couple of hours, but it was going to be a long two hours.

CHAPTER THIRTY-THREE — *Charlie*

On leaving the restaurant, Nancy and I quickly returned to the van.

"Now what?" Nance asked.

"Head north, I guess, but I must admit that I miss having Luis and Sofía already. Company is comforting and especially company that can shoot the lights out of bad guys."

"We'll do fine. California is safer."

"I know. But we have a rental car and we really should get rid of it. "And, if we do, then what? Hitch-hike?"

"Maybe we should keep on going with it."

"Possibly. But I would sure like to have some options."

"We could always go to the library."

"Hah! That's hilarious. What are we gonna do there, look up *Running from the Law for Dummies*?"

"No, sweetie. As you know, LA is a sanctuary city. Katie mentioned that the library is a supporter of that. I suspect that they can at least direct us to an organization that helps so-called illegals. Even us."

While we drove Nancy googled the Los Angeles Public Library System. We found out a couple of things. One, it's outspoken in its role as a community builder and, lately, as a critic of the White House Administration's immigration policies. Secondly, the Central Library branch is almost next door to the office of Canada's Consulate General. We would be entering a building with people sympathetic to us, located near a building with, hopefully, supportive Canadians, and all this in a sanctuary city. If there was one place we should be able to relax, even if just for a few hours while we worked out a plan, it would be there.

"Good idea. Going there should give us time to think out our next move, Nance. It seems safer there than anywhere else. Plus I don't think anyone would think to look for us there. Push comes to shove, we throw ourselves on the mercy of the consulate staff next door. Let's hope it doesn't come to that."

"I'd rather ask a librarian for help."

"Well, me too, actually. It seems that, as a group, they have been vociferous in supporting immigrants, but they may be less sympathetic to suspected murderers. If we approach a librarian, we have to be careful."

"Do you know how ridiculous that sounds?"

"Yes, you're right. But, still, I think you'd better do the talking. You're a sister and, of the fifteen hundred staff, my guess is that the majority are women. And you know how I come across to women?"

"I'm reminded of that all too often. Did you really have to ask that nice little waitress if you could lift her over your head? Seriously?"

"C'mon, Nance, she was barely eighty-five pounds and I really wanted to try."

"Never mind. Just don't do that in here if you see a skinny librarian. I'll go see what I can do."

"Just a minute. Let's do some profiling first. I think we're looking for a librarian over forty, married and wearing something plain. Jeans would be good. Ooh, if you see someone wearing Birkenstocks, I'm pretty sure you're on safe ground."

"That's insane."

"Fine. See that stretched tight woman in the black suit wearing tons of jewelry? Does she seem approachable?"

"Good God, no!"

"Well, that's my point. Look for one who feels right. An older hippy chick would be best. Go for the Birkenstocks."

Nancy just shook her head and walked away. But the more she looked, the more her instincts came into play, and the first time she felt reasonably comfortable approaching a librarian the woman was, indeed, wearing Birkenstocks.

"Excuse me, could you help me, please?"

"Certainly. What are you looking for?"

"Well, I've been listening to the ALOUD podcasts here at the library and they seem somewhat politically charged. I have to admit that some of it's a bit shocking to me. I'd like to read some more on that sort of thing, or maybe on how to protest what I'm seeing in the government. Do you have speakers or chat groups or something? Is there a library forum online?"

"We have a very comprehensive collection in the Women and Gender Studies Section. There's a lot of material there. General political protest issues such as the Occupy Movement, Black Lives Matter and human rights issues can be found on the same floor and a librarian there can direct you. You can check the calendar of events on our website or get a hard copy at the front desk. The library does host authors and speakers but, no, nothing I could define as an anti-government speakers' bureau. The library forum requires sign-up and I think you are obliged to be a librarian. I don't know for sure. I haven't been on it."

"Thank you. I'll go up to the Women and Gender Studies." Nancy turned to leave.

"What are you really looking for?"

"Excuse me?"

"No one your age asks questions like that. You have either immigrated from another planet or you are looking, without asking, for something more important than you let on. What is it?"

Nancy looked into the woman's eyes. She saw a study in neutrality. She saw no hatred, no anger, no bigotry.

"Well, one could say I come from another planet. I'm Canadian."

The woman stared at Nancy but she was processing the words and the accent. Librarians know accents. She said, "Newfoundland?"

Nancy laughed. "No, I'm from British Columbia. A good Newfie accent is a wonderful thing, but I don't have one."

"Where in BC?"

The tone had gotten sharper. A bit more interrogative than helpful, but Nancy sensed that she was being tested.

"I live on a remote island up the BC coast. I can show you on a Google map if you're interested. My husband and I built our own place there. And we've written a couple of books about it. If you want, you can look them up—*Our Life Off the Grid* and *Choosing Off the Grid*."

"Thanks. I just might. Good luck. The elevators are over there." The librarian smiled, turned and left Nancy standing and wondering what had just happened. Then she moved off in the direction of the elevators in search of a more sympathetic librarian. She was wondering if this might be more difficult than she had first thought.

CHAPTER THIRTY-FOUR — *Charlie*

I was sitting at a reading table and looking at various newspapers from Arizona and California, searching for any story published about us. There was nothing so far. That was good. But the bad news was that the library had a lot of CCTV cameras. If the FBI was employing sophisticated facial recognition software our images would be there for all to see and lead them straight to us. When you're on the run, I realized, you imagine the worst. I knew that facial recognition technology is already in wide use in China. In my paranoid state I was wondering if it was employed in this LA Library.

While I indulged my paranoia, Nancy was getting frustrated. She'd been looking for a sympathetic face or response from several librarians but it was very hard to jump from talking about a book into a conversation sharing intimate information. It just hadn't felt right so far and she hadn't gotten anywhere.

"Nancy!"

Nancy instinctively swung around. The first librarian she'd spoken to was standing there. She was holding out her hand. "I'm Deborah. Deborah Oldham. My friends call me Deb. Please come with me."

Deb led Nancy to what was obviously her office and shut the door. "Did you find what you're looking for?"

"I didn't think so. But now I'm thinking I may have . . ."

"You're on the run, aren't you?"

"How could you possibly know that?"

"The questions you asked me are very similar to questions asked by three types of people. There are the genuine politically motivated people; the incredibly clumsy and uninformed FBI or ICE undercover agents looking for leads or connections to the librarians' dissent network; and then there are the actual illegals. After I looked up your books, I suspected you were in the latter group. I'm guessing that you didn't register with Immigration and now you're worried. The quick answer is that the Canadian Consulate is practically next door and they're putting people on planes every day. No worries. You'll be fine."

"Thanks. But what if I told you that your guess, while generally correct, was missing some information and that information makes going through the consulate *not* a good idea and that we do, indeed, still have considerable worries."

"That's not good."

"No. No, it's not good at all."

"I don't need to know any more information right now."

"I understand. Thanks, anyway." Nancy got up to leave.

"Sit down. I don't want to know, but I still may be able to help. What are you trying to do?"

"Get home."

"Why not fly, or take the bus or a train?"

"The information you don't want to know would provide that answer."

"But California, Oregon and Washington are sanctuary states. The cops aren't helping ICE. You still have to avoid ICE but they're not so much interested in Canadians. All their resources are focused on Muslims and Mexicans."

"Well, in fleeing from Arizona, we managed to break a few laws that made us more than just Canadians on the run. We had no choice at the time, and we are sure a fair examination of the facts would not result in any charges, but now is not the time to end up behind bars in America. Too many innocent foreigners spend too much time in jail here. We're not taking that chance."

"Do you have a phone number?"

"Forgive me, Deb. I'm not giving it out. I can be tracked using my phone. I don't even turn it on except when it's urgent."

"I understand. Take *my* phone. I'll call you later on my office phone."

"I can't take your phone."

"Yes, you must. If it rings just say you're a friend of mine and that I left the phone at lunch. You're going to get it back to me later. I'll call in a few hours. Now go. And, if you are in as much trouble as you're suggesting, take the phone and walk out looking at it. We have CCTV."

* * * * *

Nancy and I stood outside the library entrance on Hope Street.

"The consulate is just around the corner on 6th, Charlie. Wanna go in and see what they can do for us?"

"Nope, too risky. If they'd give us refuge and then smuggle us out of the country, that'd be great. I just have a feeling that's not going to happen."

"Yeah, I agree. Well, Deb gets off work at six. She said she'll meet up with us at the Library Bar just down the street. We might as well head there now."

"You trust her?"

"Yeah. Strangely, I think I trust the profession of librarians more than most others. Why would that be? Weird, eh?"

"Not really. They're often people who love words and books. They obviously didn't get into the profession for the big bucks. So that sets them apart right off. I think I agree with you about trusting them. Them and undertakers. Undertakers consider their work a calling."

"Okay, now I could really use a drink."

We sat in the Library Bar contemplating our circumstance.

"You know, Charlie, I'm not that optimistic."

"About what? Getting away?"

"I have no idea if we'll get home safely but, think about it—at the best of times the US is divided. Remember the acrimony in the RV community when we were in Mexico quite a few years ago? The Republicans wouldn't talk to the Democrats and all that crap? That was the Bush Kerry election and it was pretty ugly. Trump is way worse. The divide is even deeper now. This doesn't bode well for their country. Not at all."

"Well, if it's bad for the country, it's bad for the world. The US is still the dog that wags the tail. And Canada is just hair on that tail."

"So that's why I'm not optimistic."

"We'll be fine."

"I'm not thinking of us. I'm thinking of our kids. I'm thinking of Leo."

"Good point. We're witnessing the ascent of the ignorant and the bigoted. It's appalling that Trumpians don't believe in climate change or science. Hell, they don't even believe in facts. They prefer alternate facts."

"Which is really stupid. Alternate means *every other one*. They mean *alternative* but they are too stupid to even use the word correctly. How did they get this way?"

"Well, I don't think you should be so hard on Americans. The education they get is often not a good one. The values they learn are money and war, celebrity and image. They watch a lot of television and eat a lot of junk food. This is a society that has been brainwashed by entertainment, propaganda and patriotism. It's hard to think straight when so many corporations, not to mention the government, are lying to you all the time. Given that, it's amazing that most Americans, on both sides of the political fence, are basically decent people."

"So what do you think *we* can do?"

"Get the hell out. Get back to our island. Stock up on beans and bullets. Watch it all implode from afar. I think things will get worse before they get better. We may as well live in a beautiful place and live peacefully while we still can."

"Well I do love it there, but I think we can do something else as well."

"What's that?"

"Well, we've witnessed firsthand some of the terrible effects of immigration policies here. We've seen the results of the rich getting rich and the poor getting more desperate. We can write a book about our experiences. At least it would feel like we are doing *something* to let people know what is really going on. Maybe it's not much but I don't have any other ideas."

"I think it's a great idea, Nance. Providing we make it home."

We were nursing a beer at the bar when Deb's phone rang. "Nancy? Deb. You at the bar? I'm on my way. Can you meet me on the street? Red Prius."

Once we were in the car, Nancy asked, "Where are we going, Deb?"

"Well, first I have to tell you something. I'm part of a small group. Nothing nefarious. A few librarians and a nurse. We're all just friends, really. But a few years ago we learned that a lot of immigrants were being detained and harassed. Some of them, who we'd come to know, abruptly stopped showing up at the library. When Trump and his Nazis came into power we started to get together to talk about it. We call it the Book Club. Anyway, we've been talking a lot and doing nothing, really. We made hats and marched and stuff but, seriously, protesting hasn't worked. We have helped a few people get out of the country by giving them some money. But we're not going to blow things up, so we've been wondering what we could do to help. Today, you showed up."

"You've mobilized a book club to save us?"

"Honestly, I have no idea what we can do. All of us but Sue, the nurse, will be at my house tonight. I'll introduce you and you can tell us your story and we'll do what we can to help. I believe what you've told me, but I have to give the others a chance to hear it for themselves. Just so you know, worst case scenario, I'll lend you my car so that you can get to San Francisco. My sister lives there. You can drop it with her. I don't know if she'll help you out or not. I'll just tell her I helped you and she can do what she thinks is best."

Dinner was fun. The women were great. Nance and I enjoyed their company and they seemed to believe in us. But, as soon as we told them we shot people to escape, without even mentioning that some were actually killed, they all withdrew somewhat. We were sure they still believed us, but being mixed up with a shooting was too much for them. They left us with hugs but, in the end, they didn't want to become more involved. We completely understood.

"I'm sorry they weren't more help."

"No problem at all, Deb. If your offer of the car still stands, we're way better off than we would've been if you hadn't offered your help."

"Yes, of course it's still offered. And so is a bed for the night. If anyone asks anything whatsoever, I'm just going to say you were couch surfers and we met at the library. So long as you get the car to my sister, it was just a generous loan. I won't report it stolen unless it's gone for more than two days. Then I'm going to have to. I'm sorry. I'm on your side but I have to limit my exposure."

"No problem. This is really good of you."

We arrived in San Francisco the following day after six and a half hours of driving. The Prius was a bit low on fuel but we had enough to get to Marin where Deb's sister lived. She turned out to be just a tad disappointing.

"Deb said that you two have done something illegal and you're wanted by the police. Why the hell she helped you, I have no idea, but I'm not an idiot liberal like she is. I've called the police. They're on their way."

"In that case," I said, snatching the keys back out of her hand, "we'll leave the car parked somewhere safe nearby. The keys will be under the mat."

We ran for the car and jumped in. Well, old white guys can't jump, and my knee *was* giving me some difficulty, but I got in as quickly as I could. We headed back down Edgewood, went left on Daffodil and left on Marion. We ended up a few minutes later at the back entrance to the Mill Valley Public Library. The car had gone full circle and was home at yet another library. We got out and walked, as calmly as we could, to the main street.

"Nance, let's look for a taxi or something."

We ended up getting on the #4 bus and it took us down to the local park and ride. From there we got a taxi to Sausalito.

"I've had enough, Charlie. I just can't keep this up. We both need some rest. Plus, I'm kinda freaked out again. Now we have the local cops after us as well."

"Maybe not. Deb's sister doesn't know what we did. She'd have trouble describing us, I think. The cops show up and there's no one else at her house. Nothing to see. The car isn't even in her name and if they call Deb she'll cover for us. What do they do? I think they put it on their day sheet and carry on. No big deal for them. So, I doubt they'll be looking for us. Worst case, an APB goes out for two suspected car thieves, soon to be forgotten."

"I guess you're right. Let's find a place to lay low and let them forget about us. And give ourselves a breather. It'd be good to have a bit of time to figure out what to do next."

"Can't use credit cards. Can't book into a hotel or show our ID. And we're running low on cash. What are you thinking?"

"We go on-line and book an Airbnb or VRBO. Something like that. Fortunately we have some money in our PayPal account. I have no idea if, or how, PayPal payments can be traced, but it's gotta be safer than using a credit card. And I bet there are tons of places for rent in Sausalito. What about a houseboat? Maybe a live-aboard boat? That might be safer. At least it's kind of off the beaten track."

"Good idea."

"Okay, I'll look for a place. And I'll text Deb to let her know where her car is. And maybe mention that she's got the sister from hell."

"I'm thinking Palm Springs would be a good place for everyone to catch a bus. Ana's going to Oregon. Where you going, Maria?"

"LA, señor. I have a sister there. She lives in South Central LA. I have been there. I can find her."

"Can't you call her?"

"I do not have her number. But I can find her."

"How?"

"She works at Compton College. I'll go there. If she's at work she'll give me her car and keys to where she lives. If she isn't, I'll wait until she arrives."

"That's crazy. Call the College. Use my phone. Talk to her. Let her know you're coming."

Dale handed his phone to Maria but Ana took it from her and found the number almost instantly. She dialed it and handed it back to Maria.

"What about you, Fahdzi? Where are you going?"

"I have not yet made a decision, Dale. I believe I'll go to the airport. This trip to America didn't work out well."

"Why did you come to Arizona?"

"I had a job interview. They invited me to come. It appeared to be a dream come true."

"Why you?"

"I'm an oncologist, Dale. I treat cancers. Some say I am amongst the best. I don't know about that, but I was offered a clinic with a large laboratory at my disposal. I was requested to take charge of the Women's Health Department. But that won't happen now."

"Why not?"

"Well, I missed the interview, although I'm sure they would reschedule it, given the circumstances. I expect they would understand that I was unavoidably detained due to the vigilantes and arrests."

"So? Why not call and tell them?"

"The main reason, Dale, is that, upon reflection, I don't believe I want to reside here in the United States. I know this is an exceptional time but, even so, there's too much hate here. I can feel it. I wouldn't be happy here. And even if I was, my family wouldn't be. I have a wife and two children. And, fortunately, I have had other offers of employment. I believe the best decision is to decline this offer. I now think that Canada might be a preferable place to immigrate."

"Canada? Polar bears and hockey? For an Iranian? Are you crazy?"

"No, Dale. I've spent time there. I interviewed there, also. I can have an excellent position there. Not as lucrative as the position in Phoenix, perhaps, but a good quality of life is extremely important to me. I could be happy there. My family would be happy. Vancouver is a beautiful city, Dale. No polar bears."

"My wife died of cervical cancer. Ten years ago. I couldn't afford the treatments."

"Yes, there *is* another aspect to my decision, Dale. At the Phoenix hospital my budget and my salary would be based partly upon how much money I could earn for them. Canada has a publicly funded health care system. People who need treatment are not turned away. I prefer that."

"If we had lived in Canada my wife might be alive today."

"That is a very difficult thing to consider, Dale. I cannot comprehend how you might feel."

I couldn't figure it out either.

As I drove, I thought about all of them catching the right buses, being alone, Maria hauling kids around, different departure times. Palm Springs wasn't going to work. It might work for them. It definitely would not work for me. I would worry too much.

"What the hell, I'll take you to LA. Why not? I have the car for a few days. Haven't been there in a while. I've got friends I can see. This way, you all get closer to where you need to go. Only two hours. Seriously, no big deal."

"Señor, they say that my sister isn't working today. She is scheduled to come in tomorrow. I can find a hotel nearby and meet her tomorrow."

"Will you permit me to pay for your hotel tonight, Maria? I would be honored. Dale, you and Miss Ana, too."

"Well, Fahdzi, I will graciously accept your kind offer as long as we don't have to share a room. Let's not let this friendship thing get out of hand, okay?"

"I'm in full agreement, Dale."

The mood felt good again. I pushed the accelerator down and the limousine surged into the chaos that was the beginning of the LA freeway system.

The place Maria chose was a casino hotel with a free breakfast. It was within walking distance of her sister's workplace. It seemed like a good choice. Everyone got out of the car to say goodbye to the family. Even me.

Maria took Ana to one side and they spoke for a few minutes. Then they hugged. Then Maria wished Fahdzi good luck, in whatever he chose to do. She told him that Canada sounded good.

Then she turned to me. She walked up to me and hugged me. She said nothing. One at a time each of her children joined her. Within a few seconds I was surrounded by hugging Mexicans. I put my arms around them, too, for a long minute. Then I had to step back. I took one last look and got back in the car. I was feeling a bit choked up and I didn't want it to show.

Fahdzi and Ana walked Maria and the kids to the entrance of the hotel and then turned back to the car. As they did, three matching black Suburbans swooped in, separating them from the limousine. Fahdzi froze. I started to get out of the car. Ana knew enough to keep walking. She literally pulled Fahdzi back into step.

Each car discharged two ICE agents. They were clad in SWAT gear and quickly ran into the hotel. I was right behind them.

"Get in the car!" I called to Ana and Fahdzi before I raced through the main door.

Maria was at the reception desk. The ICE team was beside her, but not paying any attention to her. They were gathered around a desk clerk who was showing them something on her computer screen.

"Hello, Ms Garcia, I'm Dale, your limo driver. Please come with me. I have your car waiting outside." I practically scooped up the whole family in my arms and whisked them back to the car. "Sorry, Maria. When I saw the ICE guys go in, I just reacted. It may have been stupid but I couldn't help myself. The ICE guys freaked me out. I may have overreacted."

"Thank you for what you did, señor. I was worried, too. I didn't know what to do."

"Let's go get something to drink somewhere and give the ICE people time to leave. I'll make a phone reservation and we can come back later. I'll pretend that you're my family and get you safely in the room before I leave."

"Why is this happening?" Maria started to cry.

"It may be nothing, Maria. It probably isn't. I may be just a bit on edge. But why take a chance? You're very close to getting to your sister. Let's make sure we don't screw it up now."

"Ana, what's wrong?" Maria asked.

Ana was staring straight ahead. Tears streamed down her face. She was trembling. Maria put her arms around her and held her, "What's wrong, corazón? It's going to be okay. We'll be fine."

"Those men. Immigration. They have my parents. They have guns and they look so scary. They might have gotten you, too. I thought they had. They might have gotten me and Fahdzi. I'm scared, Maria. I'm so worried about my parents. They're in danger."

"I can find out how your parents are doing, Ana. I have a friend. I'll call him. First we get everyone to some safe place away from here. I'll call then. I promise."

"Terry, Dale here. The limo driver."

"I know your voice by now, man. I know who it is."

"Right. Listen, Terry, could you do me a favor? I need to find out about some Mexicans brought in by vigilantes."

"That kid's parents?"

"Yeah. Things got a bit complicated here and she's upset. So am I, to be honest. I got an Iranian *and* a Mexican family with me as well, Terry. I drove them all to LA."

"You're not alone, my friend. It's now a *thing*."

"What're you talking about?"

"I stopped an RV earlier today. Canadian plates. Heading west on 10. I wanted to warn them about possible roadblocks. They pulled over. The Canadians had registered with ICE. They had all their papers. But, get this, they had eleven Mexicans in the back. Eleven Mexicans hiding in the back of their RV, Dale!"

"Why?"

"Same as you. Couldn't let the vigilantes get them. I told them what I knew and wished them luck. And they weren't the first. My first two were a couple of seniors who took some friends of mine with them to LA the other day. Even got away from two vigilantes to do it. Two old people, Dale!"

"Canadians fighting back?"

"Not just Canucks. My neighbor took the day off today and drove a bunch up north, heading for Vegas. Even told me he was going to do it! Like he was daring me to arrest him, or something. And he's a fucking Republican, just like you. Fucking McCain signs all over his lawn the last few years. GOP this and GOP that all the damn time. He even wears a MAGA cap, Dale. And now he's driving Mexicans up north. Explain that, if you can."

"We didn't sign up for this, Terry. We signed up to get rid of rapists and murderers and to make America great again. Honest. It was that simple."

"Well, that's the problem, Dale. It isn't simple. And simple solutions from simple people won't fix a goddamn thing. Just makes it a whole lot worse. Take a walk through Florence sometime. That hell hole isn't solving anything. Half the inmates in there are Hispanic. You know what percentage of the Arizona population they are? I'll tell you—one-third. Anyway, I'll get back to you about the kid's parents asap. Give me the details."

I found a place to pull over beside a park, in the shade, while we waited for Terry to get back to us. Maria watched her kids like a hawk as they ran around. Finally I heard my ringtone—The Ride of the Valkyries.

"Dale? Terry, here. The guy in the police uniform."

"Funny. What'd you learn?"

"Well, I'm pretty sure they're okay. No reports otherwise, anyway. They lucked out and ended up together in Eloy. But they *are* going to be deported. They haven't got a chance of coming back. No papers. Nothing. The bounty's been paid. Your kid isn't seeing them anytime soon. They aren't scheduled to be shipped out yet, but they will be soon."

"Does anyone know where they get sent? Do they have any money?"

"ICE doesn't confiscate their money or belongings but, of course, most were snatched by vigilantes, so I don't know if they have any money. Probably not. When they're deported, they go by bus from here and cross at Nogales. They're just dumped there. If they can afford a bus ticket, they can get to Hermosillo or Juarez. Hardly anybody chooses Juarez, for obvious reasons. The Mexican government will pay them a hundred bucks a month for the first six months they're back. If they're lucky they'll hook up with one of the non-profit agencies that'll help them find a place to live and a job."

"Can you get in to see them?"

"I guess so. Professional courtesy and all that. But why?"

"Give them five hundred bucks. I'm good for it. You can tell them it's from a friend of Ana's. Tell them she's okay and I'm getting her to her aunt's place in Oregon. When they get settled somewhere, that's where she'll be. Please tell them they have my word."

"What's going on with you, Dale?"

"Nothing. She's a nice kid, okay? She doesn't deserve this."

"You driving her to Oregon?"

"Hope not. If I have to, your five hundred is in jeopardy. But the Iranian is going north. He could take her. I can afford a bus ticket for her. I'll make it work."

"My friend Luis should be in LA by now. He knows some Canadians who might be able to help you get them to Oregon."

"Can you reach him?"

"Yeah. I'll get him to call you."

I turned to my passengers. I gave Ana the information about her parents and then I told them, "My guy in Phoenix is going to put me in touch with a couple of Canadians heading north. They fled the crackdown, too. I think they got out of Arizona and helped a Mexican family as well. I'd like Ana to be with someone all the way to Woodburn and it may work out that they can take her there. And, Fahdzi, you may be able to simply get on a plane and fly out. I don't know. Your choice."

"Do you think the Canadians are okay?" Ana sounded a little worried.

"Yes, I do. My guy is in a position to know. I believe him. But, it's your call."

Ana and Fahdzi looked at each other. "I can't leave Ana unaccompanied. I'll stay with her until she's safe. You've done a great deal for us, Dale. Now it seems we have the offer of another ride to further our journey. I think we should take it. Ana?"

"If you're with me Fahdzi, it's okay."

"All right, once we get word where they are, I'll take you to this couple. I'm pretty sure you could safely get on a bus here. They can't be screening for illegals at a bus station in LA. But why take a chance now? I've come this far and they shouldn't be too far away at this point. I'd feel better meeting those Canadians before you go off with them."

CHAPTER THIRTY-EIGHT — *Charlie*

We'd been in Sausalito for a couple of days. On our first day, we noticed an old lady with a familiar looking dog. He was a Portuguese Water Dog, just like the two we'd had over the years. On the second day, he came over to Nancy for a pat.

"Ooh, you're a lovely boy, aren't you. What's your name?"

While the question was directed at the dog, it was asked loudly enough that the old lady said, "Che".

"Shay?" I asked.

"No, Che. As in Guevara."

Nance, of course, busied herself ruffling the dog's ears and half hugging and scratching him. Both were happy with the exchange.

"He seems friendly," I said to the old lady. "We had two Portuguese Water Dogs but, sadly, they're both gone now. We miss them. Typically, the breed is described as mouthy. Our dogs tended to gently put their teeth on someone's hand to check them out. Your guy didn't do that."

"No, he's very gentle. Now. When he was younger, he would. . . Where are you folks staying?"

"Down in Basin 3. Rented a lovely old tug on Airbnb for a few days. It's reminiscent of our younger days when we lived aboard boats. We're on our way home to Canada. Just taking a break. Why don't you sit down? Nance and Che seem to have a love fest going on."

I introduced myself and Nancy. Grace was her name and she lived up to it. She gently took the offered seat and graciously accepted a further offer of a cup of tea. We got to talking.

Turns out Grace was in her late eighties and not getting about much these days. We managed to bump into her because she made a point of going to the Fish Shack every day, as much to give Che a walk, as to have a bite to eat.

"Well, Grace, if you'd like Che to have a longer walk sometime, you only have to ask," said Nance. "I'd love to take him for a walk. Plus, I'll pick up some groceries, too, if you need anything. Mind you, we're only here for a few days."

"That's very kind of you. I haven't been feeling at all well this past week—I would love to take you up on your offer. I live a block down Harbor Drive—1010 Cypress Place. You'll see it ahead of you when you cross Bridgeway. If you don't mind, I'll get along home now and you and Che can come whenever you want. Of course you are welcome, too, dear," Grace said to me.

She told Che to stay and he did. Then she slowly ambled back in the direction from which she'd come.

"Che seems pretty calm about all this. Mind you, he turned his head a few times to watch Grace go. Maybe you should take him for a walk and then get him back before he gets anxious. She's a very trusting woman, isn't she."

"She is, but I can see she's ill. I think she needs the help. You coming?"

"No, I'll use the Wi-Fi here. I'm still trying to figure out a way to get a set of wheels. I'm looking at YouTube to learn how to steal cars. Not as helpful as I'd like. So far, I need darkness, privacy, a portable drill, a slim jim, plus a screwdriver. And that just gets me far enough into it to get caught and prosecuted. I can imagine sitting in a car with a wailing alarm and my drill stuck in the ignition. I'm not overly encouraged."

While I was sitting in the cafe I turned the phone on briefly to try to call Ben and Katie. I wasn't able to reach them so I decided to leave a text message for Katie instead. As I was texting a call came through.

"Charlie? It's Luis. Are you still in LA?"

"No. We're in San Francisco. Sausalito, actually. Why? You okay?"

"Yes. We are fine. And Miguel is turning out to be all right. I might even like the bastard someday. He loves his son. He cannot be all bad."

"So, why'd you call? Bored?"

"No. You remember Terry, the cop?"

"I'll never forget him."

And Luis told me the story.

"Okay, here's the deal, Luis. We'd be happy to take them. No problem. But I really don't want to drive back into LA, especially as I don't have a car right now. I'm working on getting one. Will it work if I just pick them up at the bus station here? I can do that by cab. At least we have a place to bring them to. We're laying low. Had a bit of a thing getting up here and just want to take it easy for a bit."

"Are you okay now?"

"Oh yeah, we're fine. Met a great librarian in LA but her sister in San Francisco wasn't so hot. What started out as a free ride ended up in a situation. We got away, but we've had to keep a low profile since then."

After a couple more calls, it was all arranged. Some limo driver was going to drive an Iranian guy and a fifteen year old Mexican girl to join us. It all seemed so logical when I was on the phone with Luis, but not so logical when I tried to explain it to Nancy when she returned from her walk with Che, both happily tired, an hour later.

We continued to discuss the new arrangements as we headed down to Grace's house. Her place was notable because of the barrels of dead flowers out front. This old lady wasn't keeping up with the Joneses, that was for sure. I knocked on the screen door. The actual front door was ajar. "Grace? It's Charlie, Nancy and, of course, Che, in all his glory."

There was no answer so I knocked again and this time I shouted a little louder. Hearing no response, or anything at all, we went in. Grace was sitting in a chair and looked asleep. I gently nudged her shoulder and she answered something but it was unintelligible.

"Grace? You okay?"

I was pretty sure I heard her say, "No. Help."

"Nance, I think Grace is either really ill or completely whacked out on something. She obviously needs help."

"We should call an ambulance."

"Yes. You do that and look after Grace and I'll look around. See any medications? Booze? Anything that might give us a hint . . . ?"

I did a quick check and found her keys and her purse. Her desk held a lot of papers. But there was no suicide note, no medications, no booze. Grace lived cleanly but, according to the contents of the fridge, not exceptionally well.

"She has absolutely nothing in the fridge and the cupboards are bare, too, except for dog food."

"Oh, dear. Well, at least we have something to tell them at emergency."

We took Grace's car and followed the ambulance to the hospital. Grace had enough identification and insurance documents in her purse for us to get her admitted and we were able to answer everything asked of us truthfully. She was assigned a social worker when she wasn't able to sign her own consent form.

"So, you just met her today?"

"We saw her walk by yesterday and introduced ourselves today."

"Anyone else live at this address?"

"Don't know for sure, but it would appear that it's just her. No indication of any others."

"Do you know her next of kin?"

"No. But we can go back and look through her papers. Think we should? It isn't our house and, although Grace trusted us, she may have relatives who feel differently."

"Grace is extremely unwell. Her prognosis is not good. The doctors are saying pneumonia but, until the tests come back, all they really know is that her lungs aren't clear. She's pretty old and generally not in good health. They think she's malnourished. So, it's up to you. Do you think that information warrants you going through her papers to find a relative? The normal procedure is for me to get a court order. However, I'm afraid, in this case, that we may not have enough time for that."

"Okay. We'll do it right away."

We located Grace's will and checked her beneficiary. She had a daughter in Omaha, Nebraska. The daughter said she'd fly out the next day. She thanked us for our assistance and she accepted our offer to look after Che until things settled down. She didn't ask for our full names or our address. We didn't volunteer that information.

After notifying the hospital of Grace's next of kin, we went back to the boat with Che and fed him. He was anxious, but not with us. It was as if he knew Grace wasn't well, but also knew there was nothing he could do. We believed that of him because that was how *we* felt.

"I say we check Grace's place again, Nance. See if there's anyone else who needs notifying, make sure everything is left properly, lock it up, leave the key in a place where her daughter can find it and get out of Dodge. I'm a bit worried about what happens after her daughter shows up. We may end up more involved in this situation than is safe for us."

"How are we going to get away?"

"I think we should take her car."

"We can't steal Grace's car!"

"Technically, it's not theft. We promised her we'd take care of Che and we need her car to do that. We can't use public transport with a big dog. Plus, she's going to be in the hospital for at least a while and, sadly, may never get out. We can't stay here indefinitely. We have to get home. It's only logical."

"And convenient. For us."

"Right. So, call it karma. Call it destiny. Call it dog rescue. I don't care. But that's what I think we should do."

"Okay. But I'm only agreeing because of Che. And we'll make sure she gets it back, right?"

"Of course. Think we should take her jewels?"

"Charlie!"

CHAPTER THIRTY-NINE

"Ben, I got a text from your dad and mom—finally! They're staying in Sausalito for a few days to rest up. They say it's safe there and they're enjoying being able to relax. They're looking after a dog for an old lady who's in hospital."

"Oh, that's very cool. Here I am worried sick and they're relaxing and walking a dog. I told you my parents are whacked."

* * * * *

"Agents! I'm embarrassed to call you here to tell you I'm embarrassed. Actually, we should all be embarrassed. I'm looking pretty stupid to Langley right now. And I don't like that one bit." Agent Henry was addressing a room full of FBI agents in downtown Los Angeles.

"A few days ago we knew exactly where the two armed seniors, Canadian citizens, were. We know they're suspected of shooting three people in Arizona, two of whom are dead, not to mention killing another man with a putter. A putter, people! We knew what they were driving and we knew who was with them. And, incredibly, they were heading, sweet as you please, right in our direction.

"For almost two days we were never farther than one hour away from picking them up. And yet today they're not here. Their passengers have been brought in by the LAPD and the suspects got away. They just waltzed off leaving us looking like idiots. We had our heads so far up our own butts we lost them completely. Gone. Off the radar. I want that fixed. I want that fixed real quick. As of today, this case is priority number one."

"Do we have any leads?"

"According to the passengers with them, they claimed the deaths were all in self defense. Only the third killing was witnessed by the passengers. The couple is married. The male is white, about five foot nine, two hundred and twenty-five pounds, barrel-shaped, with a military-type buzz cut. He stated to the witnesses that he was seventy years old. The wife is slight, of average height; about five foot five, with white hair. Apparently she's more athletic than you might expect. The passengers guessed that she was in her early sixties. The Arizona passengers were adamant that the couple was innocent of any wrong doing."

"We don't believe them?"

"Believing is not our job. They're suspected of killing three people. We have the bodies. Our job is to bring them in. Their Arizona landlord is also a Canadian and a friend of theirs. He provided us with their names, and details of his truck that they took, as well as their residence in Canada. Immigration is sending us their passport photos.

"An item of note is that their home is on a remote island off the grid. They could easily be wackos or part of a cult. They're not using their credit cards and their phone is turned off. One thing is certain. These people know how to run. That's not a good sign—they could easily be career criminals. They're armed and definitely dangerous."

"Maybe they're not running. Maybe they're still here in LA."

"That's why I called this meeting. We just got a lead. We believe they're in the San Francisco Bay area. Probably north of the Golden Gate. We're checking it out now. Marin County police recovered a stolen Prius, abandoned after a brief police chase there.

"It appears the suspects picked up a librarian's car in LA and were delivering it to her sister in Mill Valley. The sister knew that it had been stolen and called the police. When confronted by the sister, they ran, dumped the car, and we suspect they're holed up somewhere in the area. They certainly fit the description and the timing would be right.

"All the hotels and motels we've checked so far have no record of them but we're only half done. We're doing a thorough search of other rental accommodations although it's possible they could be staying with friends. We're checking taxis, car rentals and other places they might have contacted for transportation. No leads to date. I want every CCTV in the county checked and re-checked. I'm asking the Marin County Sheriff's Office to put all their resources on alert. I want to know everything there is to know about their movements in Marin County and I want to know it now."

"Excuse me, sir. How did the sister know the car was stolen? Did the victim report it and then phone her sister a few hundred miles away to say 'keep an eye out for my car'? And then the suspects delivered it to the sister? That doesn't make any sense."

"Good point. You interview them both again. We must have missed something."

* * * * *

"Agent Henry, the Marin County Sheriff's Office called to report an incident that may be connected to the couple we're looking for. Seems some old lady fell ill. The ambulance was called and the people who were with her accompanied her to the hospital. They answer to the description of our two suspects. The report quoted the social worker at the hospital as suggesting to them that they take care of the woman's dog. If it's them, we know where they are. The address is 1010 Cypress Place in Sausalito."

"Thanks, Washington. Inform the team. We're relocating to Sausalito right away. Tell the Bay area office to coordinate with the

MCSO. Tell the Sheriff's office I want all exits from Sausalito secured. Assemble the team at the helipad. Find out from the MCSO where to land."

"Charlie, Che and I have walked all over Sausalito including the docks. Some pretty cool boats here. Especially the houseboats—some of them are amazing. But Che could really use a good run. Let's take him to a dog park where we can throw a ball for him."

"No, Nance. That Dale guy and his passengers are on their way. They could arrive anytime. I want to be ready to go. Your bag packed?"

"Yeah, but we're doing okay here right now. Maybe we should just wait and see if Grace gets better."

"Well, with some luck, she'll be fine. But her recovery's going to take a long time, most likely. And her daughter's probably here already."

"Never mind, you're right. And even if Grace is discharged, I doubt she'll be able to take care of Che right away. He may as well come with us for now."

"Either us or the daughter. As I said, she should be in town by now, but I imagine she would've gone straight to the hospital. We could walk over to Grace's house to see if she's there. Meet her. What do you think?"

"I don't think I want to take that chance, especially as we're taking Grace's car. But I *am* antsy. Why don't you come for a short walk with me and Che?"

We were about a block or two from Grace's street when the phone rang.

"You've been made."

"Dale? How do you know?"

"Well, it's either you, or there's something else pretty big going down. We just pulled off the 101 and there's a small army in Waldo at the park there. We also passed Sheriffs' cars on the exits to the freeway. My guess is that everyone is getting into position to take you down. Can you get out?"

"We can take a neighbor's car. But the only way they could know we are here is if the neighbor or her daughter told them. Possibly the social worker at the hospital. If they're putting up roadblocks they expect a car. I think we'd be walking into their waiting arms."

"Well then, unless you can swim, you're screwed."

"I can swim but that's not going to do it. Wait a minute. We'll take a boat. But, where should we go?"

"Go east. Across the bay. Head out between the Tiburon headland and Angel Island. Stay on that course, as straight as you can, to the closest point of land on the other side of the harbor. You'll be heading to Richmond. There's a yacht club, just on the right hand side of the point. Go there."

"Wow, you've got a lot of local knowledge."

"Nah, I just googled it. It's part of a chauffer's skill set these days. Once you get to the marina walk up to the main road. I'll be there soon. What do you look like?"

"Short, fat and ugly. Lovely wife and dog and we both have small packs."

CHAPTER FORTY-ONE

Henry's copter settled down in the center of the running track in Martin Luther King Park. There were a dozen police cars on Ebbtide ready to move across Bridgeway on Henry's order. With the cars in place on the freeway entrances, and Alexander Street covered farther south, the suspects were effectively surrounded.

Henry introduced himself to the Marin County Sheriff and asked if his officers were in position. "Yes, sir. We have five cars on Alexander and two at each of the freeway entrances. We've asked San Francisco police to monitor the situation in case we need help and we have two motorcycle units back on the 101 in case anyone gets through."

"Good. Is there any other way they can get out?"

"Yes, sir. If they were on a dirt bike, they could get up to the freeway but they'd have to have a car waiting there. Access to the highways is blocked. And, I suppose, they could escape by boat."

"To where?"

"To San Francisco, north past San Quentin, or Richmond."

"Okay. Just to make sure, send a car over to Richmond. We'll leave San Francisco to the SFPD and I just can't see anyone running from the law going to San Quentin but, just in case, alert them as to what's going on."

"What's the plan?"

"We're going to send in two unmarked cars to the old lady's house to scout it out. They'll confirm the targets. They'll then take up positions at Cypress and Bridgeway, leaving the parking lot open for the takedown squad. Our guys can handle entry. Your officers handle the periphery. Remember, they're armed and are known to have shot and killed. Concerns?"

"No, sir. On your signal my guys will take the lead. We'll stop on the west side of the parking lot and deploy from there. We'll leave the centre of the lot for you. All orders come from you."

"Nance, have you noticed any smallish boats with big outboards and easy access?"

"Yeah, what's your plan?"

"Steal a boat. Preferably with a Yamaha outboard. I know how to hotwire them."

"There's a nice Whaler at the end of the next dock. I think it's a Montauk. It's got a one fifteen Yamaha on the back. Center console. Think you can start it?"

"I need a screwdriver and wire cutters or a foot of wire. And maybe five minutes."

"There are some tools back at the tug. Galley drawer. Right by the stove. I'll run back and get them."

"No, I will. I haven't thought this through. I may need something else. You go to the boat. Make sure the battery switch is on, the fuel bulb is pumped, and, if you can, get the hood off the engine. I'll be there in a minute."

"Okay. Don't forget to bring the packs with you."

I arrived to see the cover off and knew that Nancy had done everything else. But she was on the dock and the dock lines were still tied.

"Nance, untie the lines."

"Che won't come."

"What?"

"He won't get in the boat."

"A Portuguese Water Dog afraid of boats? You sure he's not a Labradoodle or some wussy landlubber breed? Listen, the second I get the boat started you untie the lines, scoop Che up and step aboard. I'll catch you. No hesitation. Just grab and go."

"What if he bites me?"

"Then drop him. I'll be off the dock by then. He'll be on board."

I disconnected the wiring harness, used my newly liberated pocket knife to jump-wire the ignition and shorted the terminals of the starter motor with the screwdriver. The engine started with barely a hiccup.

A few moments later we were underway. Che had been unceremoniously bundled aboard without incident. He was nervous, but well placed in the boat, and not biting anybody. It looked like he was getting his sea legs for the first time.

Just then the engine stuttered. We were only about a hundred feet or so off the marina and I'd just pushed the throttle to half speed. My heart skipped a beat. "Did you remember to open the fuel tank air vent?"

Nancy leaped to the two big red tanks, opened the vents and gave the bulb another squeeze. A second later the big Yamaha was purring. The boat was doing almost twenty knots. It had more power but the bay was a bit choppy. Better to stay as we were. It was only five miles.

CHAPTER FORTY-THREE

"Agent Henry, our people report only one person visible in the house. She somewhat matches the description of the suspect, sixties, white hair. But she's described as having a medium to heavy build. No sign of the male suspect. There's a rental car out front."

Henry didn't like the discrepancy. His Arizona source and Rodriguez had both used the term slim or slight when describing the woman. Plus, a car rental would've been reported. He thought it was unlikely she was the female suspect.

"I'm sending Brewster. The occupant's more likely to open the door to a woman. Have her join Irving in the parking lot. Tell them to ditch the FBI jackets. Try to look like Jehovah's Witnesses. They can knock on the door. But they still need to proceed with caution."

* * * * *

"Agent Henry, the woman in the house appears to be the homeowner's daughter. She arrived last night. She spoke with the suspects two days ago. They were the ones who told her of her mother's condition. They have the old lady's dog and her car. It's a 1996 Toyota Corolla. White. We've put out an APB on it. It should show up soon."

"The car's still here in Sausalito. I'm almost sure of it, Washington. Look in the parking lots nearby. In the meantime, alert SFPD and San Quentin. I think the suspects left by boat. Also tell the agents who went over to Richmond to keep an eye out and check the marinas."

"How did they know we were coming, sir?"

"Good question. Maybe they just got lucky and drove in as we were assembling at the park. They put two and two together and, thinking that driving out was not an option, took a boat."

"How could they get a boat?"

"Lots of small boats in the yacht basin. Could've been anything. The marinas here should have security cameras. Check the ones closest to the old lady's house first."

CHAPTER FORTY-FOUR — *Charlie*

We walked out of the Richmond Yacht Club, spotted the limo almost immediately, and walked a block down the road to it. "Dale, I'm Charlie. This is Nancy."

"Pleased to meet you. And please get in. We need to get out of here. My guess is that when they don't find you over in Sausalito, they're gonna look here."

I got in the front. Nancy and Che jumped in the back. We introduced ourselves to Ana and Fahdzi as Dale drove.

"Thanks for coming, Dale. Much appreciated. But you can't be seen with us. Out of all of us, you're the only one who can go back to what you were doing before this all happened. Don't screw that up. No point."

"Actually, I agree. If I stay away much longer I'm gonna lose my job, and maybe the company reports the limo stolen, or something. I sure as hell don't need that hassle. No job, no cat food."

"Unfortunately, Dale, we have a new problem. We had a car that we borrowed but the FBI knows about it now. That car is no longer an option."

"A car's no problem. I can boost a car for you and then I should get back. There's a small airport nearby. Let's check the parking lot there. I can start just about any car, given a few minutes. What would you like?"

Much to Dale's irritation, I chose an older Nissan Pathfinder. "Dale, it's what I drive back home. Handles great. Especially in the snow. We could run into snow on the mountain passes on our way home. I'd settle for a nice Land Cruiser, but I could drive a Pathfinder to the Arctic Circle and back. It'll do the job. Plus it's a car that doesn't stand out or attract attention."

Dale gave us instructions for getting the car stopped and started and then offered us some advice. "My suggestion is, don't stay on the I-5 for too long. The vehicle's going to be reported stolen within a few hours. Maybe sooner. Usually an airport theft goes unnoticed for a few days, but this is a local air strip, and people probably come and go more frequently. This is an older car. The driver ain't rich. Could be a worker here. He could report it gone at the end of his shift. You might just have a few hours head start and then the plates are in the system."

"We'll head over to the 101. It'll be a bit slower than the I-5, but I'm thinking there'll be fewer cops."

As Nancy and I put our packs in the Pathfinder and got Che settled, Dale said his goodbyes.

"Fahdzi, you're the best A-rab I ever met. And the only one," laughed Dale.

"It's been a pleasure, Dale. I won't forget you."

"And, Ana, I'll get your parents' car fixed up when I get back. It'll be there for you, or them. Tell them I'll drive it over the border if they want."

"I'm going to miss you, Dale."

"Maybe not for long. This'll blow over. I hope. When it does, you might come back. If you do, I'll help you. You have my word on that."

To me, Dale asked, "You want my piece?"

"Thank you, Dale, but no. You need it more, just living in Arizona, than we do running from the FBI."

"You might be right about that."

166

CHAPTER FORTY-FIVE

"Agent Henry, we found the car in a marina parking lot. We have agents going from boat to boat, checking to see if anyone saw anything. So far, nothing. The security cameras are a bit sketchy. All the marinas have them, but several have them on timers so they just turn on at dusk. And not all areas are covered. But so far we have identified ten vessels that left Sausalito marinas during the time period between our first cars coming on the scene and now. Two boats headed east, the balance towards the Bay. We're lucky it wasn't a weekend."

"Concentrate on the two heading east. If the suspects were in one of those boats, where would they likely land? Let's not assume they were just trying to get away and had no further plans."

* * * * *

"Sir, the Richmond Yacht Club cameras have images of two people matching the suspects' descriptions *and* they had a dog *and* there was a Boston Whaler left at the dock that does not belong at the yacht club."

"Good. Send all our cars there. Thank the MCSO for their help. They're free to stand down. I'll write a letter to thank them personally but, right now, we have to move."

"Sir, the Yacht Club has cameras that cover the street out front. We have images of the suspects on the street, walking south-east, but we can't access the next nearest camera."

"Where's that camera located?"

"It's a residence, sir. No one home."

"And the one after that?"

"Not sure, but a block away there's a restaurant and a couple of small commercial buildings. We have our agents there now."

"Let me know if any of the footage shows them walking farther. If not, see what kind of vehicular traffic there was. See if anything stands out. It's all we have."

"They have to be heading north. They're Canadians, after all. But how are they moving around?"

"The guy didn't seem to have a problem boosting a boat. He may have stolen a car. He could've picked one up in Richmond. Maybe from the yacht club. Get hold of the Richmond Police. See if they've had a report of a stolen car in the last hour or so."

"What about a cab? It'd take some balls to wander around Richmond when they knew we were so close."

"Right. Check the taxis. See if there's a bus that went by."

CHAPTER FORTY-SIX — *Charlie*

We were on the 116 heading to Petaluma to join up with the 101. Nancy was in front, with me driving. Fahdzi was looking out the window from the back seat. Ana was also in the back, cuddling with Che, and looking somewhat pensive.

"You want our phone, Ana? We like to keep it turned off with the battery out because the FBI can track us when it's on. Or at least that's what we've seen in action movies on Netflix. If there's someone you want to make a quick call to, or text, you can do that."

"No, Charlie. Thank you. I'm just worried about Dale. He's all alone now. He's going home to fix our car. Dale's been very kind to me and my family. He's a good man. I care about him. And he hates Mexicans."

"He doesn't really hate Mexicans, Ana. People need scapegoats when life gets hard. They want to blame others for their problems. That's all it is. Dale lost his wife, worked hard all his life, ended up poor, and listened to nasty people on television. So, he sounds like he hates Mexicans, but the first chance he got to help you, he took it. I think he likes you very much and I think he's just lonely, like you said."

"He doesn't have to be lonely. He can live with us."

"Well, first you have to get to your aunt's. Then you have to get back with your family. When all that's done, and if it's okay with your parents, you can ask him. In the meantime, I suggest that you stay in touch with him, like a daughter, at least twice a week. That'll go a long way to making him feel less lonely."

"Then, yes please. I want to text Dale, okay?" Nancy passed her the cell.

"Fahdzi, I know you said you were interviewing for a position in North America, but you are still an enigma to me. Why are you even here with us?"

"Well, before we go any further into that, Charlie, why is the FBI looking for you? Don't you mean ICE or maybe even Homeland Security? I don't know much about all the different kinds of law enforcement here but the FBI is something special, is it not? To have them after you means you must have committed another crime. Am I wrong?"

"No, Fahdzi, you're not wrong. Our first encounter with vigilantes was horrific. Two armed thugs invaded our vacation home. We defended ourselves. They were killed. That makes us *suspected* murderers even though we're not murderers. I do apologize though. I should have said something about that. It's just that we know the truth and see it differently. The FBI is after two killers and we know that they're just making a mistake. Again, I'm sorry."

"I think you should be apologizing, Charlie. That's important information. Neither Ana nor I would have come had we known. Dale would not have risked our fate had he known. I have no idea why his source was so sure that you were okay."

"I suspect that his source was the local cop who investigated us, Fahdzi. I can't think of anyone else who would have had that information. His name is Terry. I don't have his number. But I understand how you must feel. I'm happy to drop you somewhere if you want. We're still happy to help you, but we just want to do the right thing. Your call."

Fhadzi turned to Ana. They looked at each other. Something must have passed between them but I didn't hear anything.

Fhadzi sat quietly for a minute and then slowly began. "At first I went with Dale to get to LA and away from the vigilantes in Arizona.

But each step we took seemed to lead to the next. I've not been afraid except when I was in prison in Florence. Maybe I should be afraid now, though. If I get arrested it will be because I'm riding with murderers. So I'm more concerned now than I was before."

"*Suspected* murderers, Fahdzi. But all the same, good thinking. Maybe you should have gone with Dale. He could've dropped you at the airport."

"I think you're right. I should have gone with him. But I told him I would accompany Ana until she was safe. After spending a brief period of time with you and Nancy, and even though you are *suspected* murderers, I believe her to be safe with you. I should have doubts but I don't. Not really. Terry was the right name to drop. We both heard him on the phone with Dale. Maybe I should be more worried but two seniors on vacation found themselves in a situation not unlike what I was experiencing, only worse. I believe you did what you had to do. Ana, is it all right with you if I take my leave and leave you with Nancy and Charlie?"

"I think I'm fine, Fahdzi. Nancy and Charlie are nice. Dale knows what he's doing—he wouldn't let me down. And I *love* Che. He helps make me feel better about things."

"So that settles it, I guess. Ana no longer seems to require my presence. I just hope I'm correct about you two. Is there another airport located nearby?"

"I don't believe there are any international airports close to us, other than San Francisco. I can drop you in Petaluma. You can get a cab or a bus back to the San Francisco International Airport. It's only an hour's drive. A cab would be best—easier and quicker."

A short time later I pulled into the Petaluma Sheraton.

"Before I depart, I'd like to know if there's anything at all I can do for you and Nancy. Or for Ana."

"I don't think so Fahdzi. Take care of yourself and be in touch when you relocate to Canada. We don't live in the city anymore but we still have connections. We might be able to help you out. And you're always welcome to visit us on our island."

Ana stood there with tears streaming down her cheeks. "Thank you, Fahdzi, for the phone and for staying with me. Right now I feel as if I'm losing my family all over again."

"Don't worry, Ana. When you get to your aunt's things will be better. And you aren't losing any family. You have two new uncles in Dale and me. Just stay in touch."

I had to keep us moving. "Sorry, guys. We have to go."

CHAPTER FORTY-SEVEN

"Sir, we have nothing. Richmond police have no recent report of a stolen car. The footage we've reviewed shows the suspects simply disappearing, although we do still have a few more cameras to check. Not much chance, though. There were a few service vehicles that went by around that time, a cab, a limousine and a couple of pickups that look like they belong to small gardening outfits. We're in touch with the cab company."

"Okay, Washington, let's hope it was the cab. Can you get anything on the other vehicles' plates?"

"Not really, sir. The cameras were black and white. Old systems. They weren't good enough to see much. The cars were moving fairly quickly. The only thing we do know is that the limo doesn't have California plates. Can't tell what they are, but they're not from California. We can send the tape to forensics for enhancement but that'll take a while."

"No. We don't have the time. If the plate isn't from California, where is it from? Odds are Nevada. High rollers are going back and forth to Vegas all the time. But, if it's not Nevada, then what? Most likely Arizona, or Oregon, I'd say."

"Sir, I saw the tape in question. It was a blur. So I'm just guessing when I say this, but I don't think it was an Oregon plate. Those plates have a tree in the middle, between the two sets of letters or digits. It's fairly distinctive and not too hard to pick out. The plate could have been anything else really, but I'm thinking Nevada or Arizona. Who takes a limo farther than that?"

"All right. Do a search of everything we have and see if we can get a better image of that limo's plates. Have them go over the footage that has already been reviewed. I want to ensure our team didn't miss something the first time around."

* * * * *

Gerry Burton got to the small community hall early to set up some chairs and attach the green and yellow flag to the podium. The usual twenty or so attendees drifted in and took their seats. Most of them were dressed in camo or green and yellow, all bearing the double X logo of the separatist movement. Once everyone had arrived, Gerry hammered the gavel to start the monthly meeting of the Medford County Committee of the Great State of Jefferson.

After the usual preliminaries, Gerry started on the agenda. "First order of business. How do we respond to the oppressive liberal states of California and Oregon refusing to cooperate with Immigration and Customs Enforcement? We've now become sanctuary states in more than name only. Our states are now defying the law and, by doing so, the Constitution of the United States!"

"Mr. Chairman, our state governments are acting like criminals by not upholding the law. Being a sanctuary state is costing us taxpayers more money for these illegals who have to be housed, fed and lawyered up. And now we're going to lose even more money if we can't rent out our jail space to ICE like we've been doing. Not co-operating means businesses will close. That means jobs, including mine!"

"Mr. Chairman, President Donald Trump just said he's going to send more ICE agents to California and Oregon. This shows he's going to deal with illegal immigrants no matter where they are in the United States. We need to support him. These illegals have to be dealt with."

"I disagree, Mr. Chairman. I don't think we should cooperate with ICE. They break the law. They act like secret police, even with white people. They can arrest people, while in plain clothes, without even identifying themselves. That's wrong. And if someone gets hurt or killed in their custody there aren't any consequences, or even any information on the public record. We're becoming a police state."

"Well, gentleman and ladies, our movement to separate from California and Oregon started because we wanted fair representation. As you know, that was way back in 1941. And, as you also know, we haven't achieved fair representation yet. And the way things are going, even if we do get it, there'll be way too many Mexicans and Muslims able to vote by then. So that means we have to protect ourselves against the mongrelization of the white race. Not officially, of course, but it's only practical. You know it is. So we have to support anything that helps us get rid of Mexicans, Muslims, Asians and Blacks. Otherwise fair representation is going to become colored representation."

"Mr. Chairman, I agree with you. Other than Winston there, we all agree. And let's remember that the Great State of Jefferson also grew out of the need for tax reform. I don't want to pay for the government not getting the job done. We've always been willing to take action. If we need something done, we should do it ourselves."

"Gentlemen, it looks like we agree to take action. Let's discuss what that action's going to look like."

And so it came to pass that the separatist movement in northern California and southern Oregon started a quasi border patrol and enforcement committee. It took a few months to get organized, but it was well received by the membership. Meetings were held in small towns in both states. Not everyone was in total agreement with adopting this militia action, but all agreed that something needed to be done and they were the ones to do it.

"You guys hungry? Looks like a quaint little diner up ahead."

We pulled in, found a booth, and settled into finding something greasy and hot. Ana excused herself and went to wash her hands.

"I like that kid," Nancy said. "She definitely has her head screwed on right. She looks pretty mature for fifteen. Acts it too."

"Che loves her and I really like her, too. I hope her aunt and uncle are going to be good to her."

Two rough looking guys came in, taking a booth close to the door. Both were wearing camouflage and ball caps with some kind of double X logo. Smidge weird. A little threatening. But I knew I was definitely in a paranoid state of mind so I just took note and tried to relax as I turned back to the menu. At least they weren't MAGA hats. They had to be locals. The pickup trucks with dogs in the back gave that away. Local guys with dogs. No big deal.

"Whoa, girl! What you doin' here? C'mon, come sit with us."

Ana's wrist had been grabbed on her way back to us. It wasn't violent. Mostly just rude. I watched carefully but, for the moment, I would leave her to contend with it. She snatched her arm back and took a step away. She looked at the two men and continued towards us. I breathed a sigh of relief.

"Hey, darlin', c'mon. Burger's on us."

"Bradley Turner! You leave that girl alone, you hear me?"

The older waitress had witnessed the brief interaction and had risen to Ana's defense. And the short-order cook leaned his beefy face through the pass through window. They knew the men and were defending their turf, more than Ana, but it was good to see anyway.

"Oh, keep your panties on, Edna. Just flirting for fuck sake. Give us two cheeseburgers and fries with all the trimmings. To go. We got things to do."

"You okay, Ana?"

"Sure. Why not? Stupid pigs are all the same. We have rude men in Arizona, too."

"Well, sometimes they can be more than rude."

"I know, Charlie. My parents told me. And I have a friend who was raped. I'm careful. But I suggest we have the cheeseburgers. They seem to come highly recommended."

It was good to have a break from the car and the cheeseburgers were delicious, but Che needed a break as well, and it was getting on. We paid and left as soon as we'd eaten and headed out to the car.

"Hey, old man. How much you want for the Mexican?"

We had company in the parking lot. And they were coming in our direction.

"Nancy, you and Ana get in the car. Get it started. I'll deal with them."

"There're two of them and they look mean."

"Please. Just get to the car." I turned to face the men.

They *did* look mean. And it also looked like Ana was not their only interest. They both took positions in front of me.

"What you doing with a spic, old man?"

"Well, she's Mexican-American. And she's my granddaughter. But, more to the point, what's it to you?"

"You ain't Mexican."

"My daughter-in-law is."

"Prove it. I wanna see some ID. Hers *and* yours."

"Not gonna happen. Why not just leave us alone. This can only end badly for you. You don't want that now, do you?"

"Whoa, old man. You got some balls. You gonna take us both, are you? I'd sure like to see that ever happen."

"Really? You want to see that?"

"Yeah, motherfucker, I want to see that."

"Okay, then. Tell me when you're ready."

As the mouthy one was about to tell me that he was ready I threw a left hand as fast and as hard as I could. I'm old, and not as strong as I was, but I had the element of surprise. And I know how to throw a punch. He took it square on the nose. I saw blood. He saw nothing at all. He was out cold. I looked over at the second guy.

"I understand. You're wondering if you should continue the fight or attend to your friend. I suggest you take care of him. I don't need any more hassle. And I'm sure you don't. Let's just end this."

He looked at me, looked at his friend and then back at me. "Fuck off."

"Sounds good to me."

Nance took the wheel and drove us away. I was a little shaky after the altercation. When I felt the adrenalin start to subside I looked up the logo we'd seen on their caps.

"They're separatists. I just looked up that hat insignia—the double X means the area they call the Great State of Jefferson has been double-crossed. They're part of a movement for a separate state in northern California and southern Oregon. They're kind of a mix of right wing nut-bars, white supremacists and militia—the equivalent of vigilantes in other parts of the country. They're pro-Trump, anti-immigration and basically a bunch of red-neck bigots. They've been more active, and a lot more visible, since Trump made it to the White House."

"Charlie, that wasn't politics back there. That was just plain old parking lot bullies looking to push people around. It started when they saw Ana just because she's Mexican."

"Mexican, schmexican. Sorry, Ana, I don't mean to embarrass you, but you're an attractive young woman and they would've hit on you whether you were Mexican or not. That was sexism, not racism."

"Who cares? It's all the same in the end. It's either hate or bigotry or prejudice or something. I don't care what you call it, it's wrong. I think it's evil. And I blame President Trump."

"How can you blame Trump, Ana? He wasn't there."

"Well, that's just it. He kinda was. The things he said in his campaign speeches have given permission for all this. The vigilantes in Arizona believe the terrible things he says. They think they're allowed to act like assholes. These guys just take that kind of thing and run with it. They're made legitimate by Trump. They're all the same."

"Well, to play the devil's advocate, some would argue that immigration needed to be controlled. That it's out of hand. That radical measures are needed. I'm not supporting that, but I *am* saying that a lot of the US population, in their magnificent and willful ignorance, voted for Trump to make America great again. Sometimes democracy makes mistakes. In other words, this just might be the new America for now, like it or not."

"I don't like it."

"And, thank God, the majority of Americans don't like it either. I think, Ana, there *is* room for hope but it might take some time."

We traveled up the coast for a while, keeping to the speed limit. After we stopped to give Che a brief walk, I took the wheel again. I passed a few cars. A few cars passed us. Then things got weird.

"There's a truck behind us, Nance. Right on our tail. High beams. I'm going to slow down and let him pass."

When I slowed, the truck pulled out to pass and raced up ahead. I knew instantly that it was the same two guys from the parking lot. I dropped back a bit farther. If they pulled over, I was going to drive past them and then go like hell. I didn't get the chance. Another vehicle with high beams came up behind us. It appeared that they were working together. With the first truck ahead of me and the second one behind me they could slow me to a stop. Stopped, we would have even more of a problem than we did right now.

I had two resources the other drivers didn't know about. I was driving a stolen car so smashing it up was not a problem. And, more importantly, we had the .45.

"Nancy, get the .45. I'm going to slam on the brakes. Ana, brace yourself and hold on to Che. When I do, Nance, hand me the gun. I'm going to jump out and shoot them. Two in the windshield to get them down and then I'm going to run up and shoot the front tires."

"I'm a better shot. You're a better driver. I'll do it. Just don't leave without me."

"Okay, you're right. Ready?" Nance nodded. I hit the brakes. The big pickup behind us also braked but still hit us with a strong thud. It didn't sound like any real damage was done. Nance was jumping out as we were still moving, slipped on the gravel shoulder because of the impact, and rolled down out of sight. I held my breath. I couldn't see her. Then I heard two shots ring out, each a fraction of a second apart. I waited for her. And waited. Then I saw her stand straight up, calmly pump a few more slugs into the tires and jump back in beside me.

"Hit it!"

By this time the first truck had slowed to a halt two hundred feet or so ahead. I could see by their back-up lights that they were coming towards us in reverse.

"Nance, those guys up ahead are moving backwards towards us. I can fly at them and veer around them. They won't be able to get going forward fast enough to block me. Shoot them as we go by."

"If you stop, I'll shoot their tires."

"They could be armed. I'll stop a car length ahead. Just open the door and shoot their windshield and grill. That'll help stop 'em."

I kicked up the high beams as I accelerated towards the truck. They must have thought we were going to ram them because they braked. I turned hard left and slammed on the brakes just past their vehicle. Nance opened her door, leaped out, took a stance and fired multiple rounds. When the gun clicked empty, she jumped back in. We took off. I must've hit a hundred for at least a minute before I slowed enough to determine they weren't following us.

"That felt good!"

"What?"

"Shooting bullets into that truck. I guess I got carried away, but at least the last two rounds went into the radiator. There's gotta be a hole in it, for sure."

"Wow! Dirty Nancy. Did it make your day?"

"Yeah, punk, I was feelin' lucky!"

CHAPTER FIFTY

"What happened to you two dickheads?" Gerry asked. "Saw your truck down at Macy's garage."

"Two old psychopaths almost killed us last night. They shot at us, shot out the tires on our truck and did the same to Billy and Ryan. Fucking assholes coulda killed us."

"Police informed?"

"Yep. They were the first ones on the scene. Didn't seem too upset about it, either."

"Not everyone agrees with the movement, Brad. You know that. They hassle you?"

"Nah. Just asked for a description of the perps and the vehicle and phoned it in."

"Who was it?"

"Like I told ya. Two old psychos and their dog. And a teenage Mexican girl."

"So, you got pretty close to them to see all that. What did *you* do?"

"Nothin', Gerry. Nothin'. Saw 'em at the diner, flirted with the girl and pissed 'em off, I guess. That's all."

"So, how did you end up all the way up there?"

"We were going that way. Billy and Ryan were following. We got ambushed by them."

"You were chasing them, you fucking moron. I know you were. Brad, you're fucking stupid. You hassle some old guy and his family and he takes you out. Good on him. You shouldn't even be in the militia. You know why? You're too fucking stupid. You and your friends are out of rotation from now on. You got that? And one more word on the matter and you're out of our committee, too. You hear me?"

"Fine. We don't need your fucking Boy Scout troop, anyway. Fuck you, old man."

Gerry Butler glared at the two younger men and turned away.

"What're we gonna do now, Brad?"

"Get Ryan and Billy. We're gonna find the two old fuckers and hand them over to ICE. We'll be heroes."

"I don't wanna get shot."

"We don't do the arresting, shit for brains. Call your ICE guy, tell 'im we know where those freaks are and tell 'im they shot at us. Don't forget to let him know they got a Mexican girl with 'em. You can say we think they're human traffickers. We'll call again when we find 'em. In the meantime, get ahold of anyone who'll help us look for them. It was a light-colored old Nissan Pathfinder. Three people and a dog. Heading north. They could be half way to Portland by now."

"We got some sympathizers up in Coos Bay. A few more near Salem. You want I should call them?"

"Yeah. Do it. Let's find those fuckers."

* * * * *

"Agent Henry, we may have something. Oregon State police reported an incident last night. Shots were fired at two pickup trucks. The shooter disabled the vehicles and shot up the cabs of both trucks. Kind of looks like road rage, except for one thing."

"What's that?"

"The shooter was a passenger in a vehicle. Female. White hair. She rolled out of her vehicle, took out the tires and then shot at the people in the first truck. The really cool part was that she did it again with the second vehicle. We have ourselves a real Bonnie and Clyde, sir."

184

"You think it's cool that civilians were shot at, agent?"

"No, sir. Of course not. Apologies, sir. It's just that, well, the two pickups held four members of the Great State of Jefferson militia. They've recently mobilized to basically hassle foreigners, sir. Or, rather, anyone who looks like me. Deeply pigmented, you might say. They're aligning themselves with ICE and acting like the vigilantes in Arizona. I'm guessing they picked on the wrong couple. Just saying."

"Keep that kind of commentary to yourself, Washington. If they were our fugitives they sure know how to find trouble. Let's move. We've now confirmed they're heading north. Advise the Portland office, but instruct them not to notify ICE. So far, this is just an FBI case. Let's not make it any more complicated than it has to be."

"Mr. Barnes? I'm Agent Henry. It's nice to meet you. Have they been treating you well?"

"Not really. I've been arrested without charges. That can't be legal. And I'm in jeopardy of losing my job if I don't get back to work so, no, I would say I'm *not* being treated well."

"Well, Mr. Barnes, you've not been arrested. You're only being held in police custody. I'm sure it'll all be over soon. Just answer a few questions and you can soon be on your way."

"What do you want to know?"

"Where are the Canadians and why did you help them?"

"I have no idea what you're talking about."

"That's interesting, Mr. Barnes. May I call you, Dale? Well, I will anyway. I know just about everything so far, Dale. You, the Iranian, the Mexican family, the kid. Ana isn't it? And the Canadians. And I was there in Sausalito. You were good there. Made us look pretty stupid, but I'm not one to hold a grudge. It's all's well that ends well, right? So, where are they, Dale?"

"What Mexicans? An Iranian? You must have me mixed up with someone else. And maybe I need a lawyer answering for me if you're going to keep talking like this. What do *you* think, Agent Henry?"

Henry looked at me. I knew he knew that I wasn't easily intimidated. Worse, for him, he knew time was on my side. Stalling worked for me but not for him.

"Dale, we have your car. We're running it through forensics right now. We'll get DNA proof of who was in it. You know that, right?"

"Yeah. You'll get Iranian DNA. You'll get Mexican DNA. Maybe DNA from my cat, Rufus, too. What of it?"

"In an obstruction of justice case, it'll be relevant."

"I'm not obstructing justice."

"I think you are, but I *do* believe you don't think so. So, I'm going to cut you some slack, Dale. You have my word. I'll even write this down and sign it. I will not prosecute you for anything—*if* you tell me what I need to know. And tell me now."

"Well, let's pretend I had something and didn't know I had it, like you said. I'd have to talk for hours before I mentioned it, wouldn't I?"

"Don't be a smartass, Dale. My good mood, and my willingness to keep you out of this mess, has a very short window for acceptance."

"Well, I really don't know any Canadians. And if I did, how would I know where they are or where they're going?"

"Here's the deal. We know you saved a fifteen year old girl from some vigilantes. We know you decided to drive her out of Arizona to get her someplace safe. You like this kid. You have a young girlfriend, whatever."

"That would make me a pedophile. You callin' me a pedophile, Agent Henry?"

"Of course not. My apologies. Not a girlfriend. Just a friend. Noted. But, you took her out of state. We know it's not kidnapping because, well, we just do. But it could be a legitimate charge. You know that, right? We know her parents have been deported to Mexico. You saved the kid. I get that."

"I didn't save her. She saved herself."

"Fine. So then she hires a limousine to drive her to LA? You expect me to believe that?"

"No. I decided to drive her to LA all on my own. I'm a nice guy."

"And, on the way, you pick up a Mexican family. Just happened upon a family of Mexicans and took them, too?"

"I didn't. Ana found them. And, as you already know, she found an Iranian guy, too. They were all in the bus station in Phoenix. I was taking the kid to the bus station when I found myself surrounded by foreigners. What was I supposed to do?"

"So, what happened? Why not drop her and get on with your day job?"

"Because I heard that buses were being pulled over by vigilantes before they crossed over into California. I decided to drive them myself. Safer. But I don't think that's a crime, is it? Should I have handed them over to idiots in pickups looking for the bounty? You think I should hand a fifteen year old girl over to vigilantes?"

"No, Dale, I don't. I think you did the right thing. That's what makes this question so hard to answer."

"What question?"

"Why would a decent guy, who cared about a young girl, hand her over to known killers?"

"I don't know any known killers. What the hell are you talking about?"

"Furthermore, how did this seemingly good guy know where to find these known killers? And why would he thwart FBI efforts to apprehend these killers? What's motivating Dale Barnes?"

I was upset. I had no idea the Canadians were murderers. I thought they were just running from ICE and the vigilantes, like Ana and Fahdzi.

"I didn't know . . ."

"I believe you, Dale. I don't think you did know. You'd have to be pretty callous to hand over a little girl to killers. What was going on Dale?"

I was just about to explain when I realized that Henry had tricked me. My intent was to protect Ana and now I was about to give information that might endanger her.

"I don't trust you. How do you know they're murderers?"

"The Pinal County Sheriff's Office and the Yucca Valley Police Department have reported three dead vigilantes. Everything points to the Canadians. Two of the bodies were recovered adjacent to their Mesa residence. I can't prove they did it, Dale. Not yet. But there is no doubt that the two Canadians were present both times when these people were killed. We *can* prove that much already. So . . . how did you get in touch with them?"

"I got a phone call from a guy called Luis. He told me the Canadians got him and his daughter out of Arizona, just like I was doing. He offered to get me off this crazy underground railroad and drop my people with others heading north. He vouched for them."

"I'm going to need his full name."

"I don't know it. I just know him as Luis."

"How'd he get your number?"

"He didn't say. I didn't ask. Has to be someone we both know, I guess. Anyway, I was already in LA, wondering how to get Ana safely up north."

"Why up north?"

I knew that this was the question where there was no turning back. I needed more time to think.

"How did you know the Canadians were in Sausalito? I doubt that Luis called *you*?"

I had just answered a question with a question. Henry would know the answer was important, because I'd avoided it, but he didn't press yet. He kept things conversational.

"We had them on the radar all the way to LA. Then they disappeared so we put out an APB. Seems they had stolen a car and got as far as Marin County when they were spotted. They went to ground for a few days. We kept an eye on everything up there. Eventually we got a lead that led us to Sausalito. That make you feel better, Dale? I hope so, because now I want an answer to my question."

Three bodies. Stolen car. Hiding in Sausalito. It all added up.

"I guess I'm not in a good position to bargain, Agent Henry, but I may as well be frank. If I don't get some promises from you, I'm going to clam up. And, when I say promises, I mean in writing."

"You could make things worse for yourself."

"Not really. You just said that you believed me. I didn't know the truth about the Canadians and you know I didn't. So, basically, I'm guilty of nothing, except maybe obstruction of justice, but I don't believe for a minute you could get me on that. I don't want much, Agent Henry."

"What assurances?"

"Ana and Fhadzi are one hundred percent innocent. They are just ordinary people caught up like I was. They should not only be kept safe and set free, but Ana needs to get back to her family. ICE will send her to juvenile detention. Then she'll be dumped in Tijuana or Nogales when she turns eighteen. She wouldn't last a week. I want your word that ICE does not get her. I want that in writing."

"I'll do that. I don't want to see that happen either. But time is of the essence for me right now, Dale. I just don't have time to get that all vetted by the department's lawyers. But you *will* get it. You have my word. No charges on anything to date. Ana and the Iranian included. No promises after today. Further, I promise I *will* get Ana to her family. I'll keep that promise if I have to do it myself and use my own money. Believe me or not, it will all be in writing. Just not now."

"It should be an easy promise to for you to keep—getting Ana to her family. Ana has an aunt in Woodburn, Oregon. They're headed there. My guess is they're getting close already. And, no, I don't have a name or an address."

Henry turned to leave, took a step towards the door and then stopped abruptly. He turned, extended his hand to me, and said, as we shook hands, "I keep my word, Dale. Ana and the Iranian will be safe. You can count on it."

CHAPTER FIFTY-TWO — *Charlie*

"Ana, Charlie and I've been talking about something." Nancy said. "You and Che have really bonded. I can see that he's very fond of you."

"Yes . . ." Ana replied hesitantly, a little excitement creeping into her voice.

"Well, we think Che might be better off staying with you, rather than coming to Canada with us. There's still the possibility that Grace will be able to take him back, but that'll become less and less likely as time goes on. How would you feel about keeping Che for now, if it's okay with your aunt?"

"Really? That'd be totally awesome. Che, you're going to stay with me!"

I was glad that we were able to do this for Ana. And Che, as well. I knew Nancy was disappointed to lose him, but we both knew it was for the best.

"Charlie! I just saw a truck with two men like the ones who were after us earlier. Same kind of hats."

"Where is it, Ana?"

"Ay Dios mio—they're coming!"

"It's okay, Ana. We're ready. Nancy, make sure the gun is loaded. The extra clip is in the bag. Take the old clip out and put in the extra bullets from the little bag."

"I don't know how."

"Me, neither but there has to be a little lever or something. Maybe two. One would be the safety, the other ejects the clip. Do your best."

The truck Ana noticed had caught up with us, but they were staying back, keeping the same distance between us. I estimated that they were about a hundred yards behind us. Hard to see their faces but close enough to see that the passenger was on the phone."

"My guess is we've been made. The Jefferson militia is calling in our position."

"Who to? That first bunch of idiots is hours back. Who do you think they're calling, Charlie?"

"Police, maybe."

"How far to Woodburn?"

"We just passed Grand Ronde. If I go right, we head to Salem but, if they *are* calling the cops, we're driving right to them. I think I should go left and follow the 18. The road is narrower but maybe I can lose the tail and then take a side road."

"Okay. I have the clip out. How do I put the new one in?"

"I don't really know. All I do know is that once it's in half way, you palm-slap it into place so that it definitely catches. Just don't hit the damn thing so hard you accidentally shoot us."

It snapped nicely into place. Nancy was sweating. So was I.

"You guys are a lot better shooting at people than loading guns."

"Thanks, Ana. But we're just starting out as criminals. It's all new to us."

"Nancy looked pretty mean back there."

"Oh, I've seen her mean before. Just not armed at the same time."

"Okay, guys. I have a loaded gun and I've reloaded the clip. We're ready to rock and roll!"

"Rock and roll?"

"Isn't that what they say?"

"I think it's 'lock and load' but it really depends on the movie and which action hero is involved. I'm pretty sure you can make up your own wisecracks."

"Ooh, good! Then we're ready to 'heat and serve'. What do you think?"

"Keep working on it."

When I took the turn at 18 and headed north, the passenger in the truck behind us got back on the phone. He was brief.

"I think he just reported in again. They know we're on 18 headed north. It would be too coincidental for more militia to be up ahead, but some local cop might be."

"What do you want to do?"

"I think we should head into Sheridan. If they follow, I'll try to lose them by driving like hell. The idea is to get back onto the highway and head in a different direction. They think we're heading north. I can head south or east if I can lose them long enough to get out of sight."

I took the exit at Sheridan and hit the gas. I was flying as I entered the small town. I was an accident or a speeding ticket waiting to happen and my followers were reluctant to keep up. I was soon four blocks ahead. From then on, it was by the seat of my pants. I took a left as I passed the high school and found myself in a residential neighborhood. Grid pattern. That meant I could afford to go two blocks before the truck made the same turn. I took a right at that point, went one block west and then I made a left.

At this point, they should be as confused as I was. I was thinking they would slow up some, it being a highly populated area, so hopefully they wouldn't come as deep into it as we were. I took the next right on a street that angled. Instinctively, it seemed to me that we would be less visible on a street that deviated from the grid pattern.

Logic suggested they would soon realize that finding me in town was harder than waiting for me back on the main road. I turned onto the road we'd come in on and went back out towards the 18. I blasted back to the highway but, instead of taking the turn that led north, I continued on the same road in an easterly direction into an area of rural farmland.

They may have seen us. They may have tried to follow. I don't know. All I knew is that we were hurtling into farm country and no one was visible in the rear view mirror.

"Good moves!"

"Or lucky. We'll see. I think we should use the phone and see where this road leads. If we can get into Woodburn by a back way, we're less likely to encounter roadblocks or militia. At least until we get to Ana's aunt's place."

"No one knows we're going to Woodburn or Ana's aunt's. If we can get in the back way, we should be good."

"Well, the FBI is on our tail. They know we're heading north. We're Canadians running for home. Not rocket science. They may also know we have this vehicle. Remember that Dale said we probably only had a few hours head start."

"And the guys I shot at may have reported us."

"Still, I don't see anyone knowing where we're headed. They may know us when they see us, but they won't know we're coming."

CHAPTER FIFTY-THREE

"We lost 'em, Brad."

"Where?"

"Sheridan."

"So they're still headed north. We're an hour out of Salem. Can you meet us there?"

"Yeah. Instead of Salem, though, why don't we meet out on the freeway heading north? You know the Volcanoes Baseball Stadium? It's less than a mile north of the main overpass into town. Just pull over on the shoulder. We're in a lifted F250. Red tailgate."

"Okay. Got it. I know the place."

* * * * *

"Brad? Slick, here. You still want information on a Nissan Pathfinder?"

"Sure do."

"The detachment's been alerted by the FBI to look out for a Pathfinder driven by two Canadians. The car's also carrying a teen and a dog. They believe it's headed towards Portland. They're trying to find out exactly where. Our officers are supposed to intercept them. We just don't know where that's going to happen yet."

"Let me know when you do, okay? We're heading north right now, but we're still a few hours south of Portland."

"You'll get there before the FBI does. They're at least four hours out, they said."

"That's good. Tell the ICE guys. Tell 'em the Jefferson militia called you and alerted you, okay?"

"Roger that, cuz".

* * * * *

"Washington, do we have a location yet?"

"Yes, sir. The aunt lives on Grant Street a few blocks from Front. Corner of Fourth and Grant. Four nine six. Small two storey.

"Okay. Tell them not to approach the house. Have the area surrounded. Four block radius. Use local cops on the main streets. No more than two cars. We have Portland sending four teams. Make sure the local officers look like they're on normal duty. No guns drawn. No sirens. Have some female agents get neighbors out of the way. Keep it totally discreet. These runners are smart and careful. Let's not lose them again."

* * * * *

"Brad, we have the location. Spic-town. Four nine six Grant. But our instructions are to stay at least four blocks away. We can't go closer. I told ICE and they said that they can go wherever they want. They thanked you for the tip, but I don't think I can help you much more. If the FBI and ICE clash, the shit is going to fly. I have to keep low on this. I'm already in trouble, I think, for telling ICE."

"Don't worry. It'll go down okay. If it goes bad, tell them I asked you to contact ICE before you were instructed not to. I'll back that up."

* * * * *

"Sir, we just received a report from a local cop on an undocumented Mexican female from Arizona coming to Woodburn. That's no surprise, but it seems the FBI is on her tail. So it might be something big."

"A female illegal running from the FBI is interesting. Why didn't they inform us?"

"I checked and there has been no notice to us whatsoever. Nothing. Not even a phone call. They're cutting us out, I guess. Should we send over a team?"

"No. We have enough to do. If it's FBI business, it's not necessarily our business, but I am pissed at the lack of respect. Where's the courtesy, Domingo?"

"The courtesy, sir, came from the Jefferson militia. They told the local cops and specifically asked that we be informed. We're getting respect from all the wrong places, sir."

"Those Jefferson assholes. So, the militia knows, the locals know and the fucking FBI knows. Maybe the press even knows. We're going to look stupid, if we don't already. Where's the target?"

"Seems downtown. Fourth and Grant."

"Good. We have an undercover team down on Front. We have a guy in a kitchen, too, don't we? Cooking tacos and shit? Can he get away? Alert them all. Have them walk up and down the street. Tell them not to get involved. But, if something goes down, have them report in immediately. I want to know what's happening, even if it's just to cover our asses."

"Sir, we have to keep our guy in the kitchen regardless of how hot it gets. But he can act as a lookout for the two street covers."

"Oh, Domingo, that's tortured, you know that? Just do your job. Skip the humor. Doesn't work for you."

"Ana, where are we going? What's the address?"

"I don't know the address, but I was there years ago. I was ten. But I know what it looks like."

"That will help if we get close, but do you know where in Woodburn your aunt lives? The neighborhood?"

"She owns a restaurant. There are more Mexican restaurants near hers, but hers is the best. It's downtown. I don't know how to get there, but there are train tracks running down the main street. When we find the restaurant I can find the house because she walks to work every day."

"That should do, Ana. Is she expecting you?"

"No. I don't know her phone number. It was on my cell, but, as you know, I had to leave that behind. Plus, I didn't want to worry her."

"That's pretty sweet, Ana, but you'd better call her now. Here's our phone. Here's the battery."

"They only have cell phones. The numbers aren't listed."

"Damn. Then phone the restaurant. See if she's there. That'll have to do. Where does your uncle work?"

"He's a fireman but he works at the restaurant too, sometimes. So he might be home. I don't know the name of the restaurant."

"Okay. First you look at the list of Mexican restaurants on Google. If that doesn't ring a bell, try one after another until you find your aunt's. We'll head downtown anyway and you'll likely remember which one it is if you see it."

Ana stared at the phone, "La Mesa Mexican Restaurant. That's it! It means table. I remember."

* * * * *

"Rosa? Rosa Perez?"

The woman was in her mid-fifties, well dressed, with the appropriate deportment to go with it. She looked like the business owner she was.

"Yes? How can I help you?"

"My name is Charles Moon and I have just come from Arizona. My wife and I have your niece, Ana, with us. She's just outside in our car. I wanted to come in first and make sure it was okay before I brought her in."

The woman's face lit up, her head spun towards the front of the restaurant. "Where is she?"

"Rosa. Look at me. Is it safe to bring her in here?"

"Of course, of course. Why wouldn't it be?"

"Because we think you're being watched."

"Watched? Who would be watching us? Por qué?"

"Do you know what happened in Arizona?"

"Si, my brother called. We've been worried sick."

"Well, there's a bit more to the story now than what your brother told you. But let me bring Ana in."

I went to the door and motioned Nance and Ana into the restaurant. Rosa and Ana hugged and Rosa began to tear up.

"Rosa, I'm sorry to interrupt, but we have to go and we need to sort out a few things first."

"Of course, of course. Come. Sit down. What can I get you?"

"Nothing, thank you Rosa. No time. There are police officers parked at both ends of Front Street. They may be looking for us. Getting out of the truck exposed us and so they may be making moves. We just don't know."

"But, why señor? Why would they want you?"

"Long story. Ana can fill you in. But we are fugitives. I need to know that you want Ana to stay with you and you'll take care of her."

"Of course. Of course I want her. She is family. I love her."

"Good. That will have to do. That and seeing Ana's face light up when she saw you. This is way too quick, but it feels all right. Okay, next, can you take our dog, Che? He and Ana are close. He's a good dog. If you don't want him, we'll take him but, for now, he's better off with you and Ana."

Rosa looked at Ana for confirmation and said, "Of course. We'll take care of Che and love him, won't we Ana."

"Finally, please don't lie for us. Don't cover anything up. Tell the truth to anybody official who asks. Lying won't help us and can only put Ana and you at risk. Promise?"

Rosa was a bit hesitant to agree. Not because she wanted to lie, I inferred, but simply because she was confused by the request. "What are you talking about? Who will ask questions?"

"Maybe ICE. Maybe the local police. Definitely the FBI. We're on the run, Rosa. The government is after us. We're innocent. They think otherwise. It could end badly and, if I'm right about the cops on Front Street, it might happen here. We have to get away quickly."

"You can take my car."

"Thank you, Rosa, but no. That would just implicate you. What I need to do is steal someone else's car. Someone with no connection to me and, ideally, none to you."

"Can you ride a motorcycle?"

"Yes. What are you thinking?"

"Our delivery boy rides a motorcycle. It's parked out back. He leaves the keys in it because he's in and out all the time making deliveries. He even has two helmets because he picks up his girlfriend after work. I can ask him to take my car on a delivery or something."

"I hate to steal a kid's bike, but I'm tempted."

"Don't worry. I'll promise him a new one. He's a good boy. If this helps you, I'm okay with that. You have done so much for our family. You have brought Ana safely to us."

We hugged Ana while Rosa went to instruct the boy to take her keys and go and pick up her grocery order at the wholesalers. As soon as the kid left, I got on the bike and fired it up to familiarize myself with it. Nance went to the car to get our packs and collect Che. Ana stayed with her aunt. Rosa didn't want to take her eyes off her.

CHAPTER FIFTY-FIVE — *Charlie*

As I was getting on the bike, Ana came running out the back door of the restaurant, "Charlie, Charlie, some nasty looking guys, like the guys on the highway, are walking towards Nancy. She's in the car. I don't think she can see them."

I hit first gear and spun the bike around in the parking lot. I raced down the lane and made the turn, heading for Front Street. I slowed to a crawl as I passed the police car parked on the corner, and then slowly accelerated to the speed limit. Cops always check out bikes, but I was pretty sure I only got a passing glance.

I could see the two men almost level with the Pathfinder as Nance got out. I was about a hundred feet away. Che was watching them intently. Nancy closed the car door and glanced toward the restaurant. At the same time she reached for something in one of the packs. I knew what she was thinking. I accelerated. The two guys also knew what she was going after and they lunged to stop her. Che reacted by leaping for the first guy and sinking his teeth deep into the man's thigh. I could hear his scream over the bike's engine. Nancy was falling back against the truck as she saw me come into view. I was traveling quicker than she expected.

Without braking I hit the second guy with my right foot extended into his lower back. The impact was significant. He flew ten feet forward about a foot in the air. His face came to a sickening halt on the back left tail light of an old Ford sedan.

"Get on!"

"What about Che?"

"Nance! We have to go! Ana will get him. C'mon!"

My memory of the area from Google maps indicated a green space that followed a creek for a long way. All I had to do was get to the end of Front Street and turn right. That got me to a park-like area and there was access from the road. I took it. We were heading down a trail in an open field in the direction of a forested area. I knew there was a creek there, just from the slope of the ground.

The bike was perfect except for the tires. They had a compromised trail bike tread that had been worn down a bit from the kid's delivery work. The trail was relatively dry, and it posed no problem, but I knew that I would have trouble in mud or slippery conditions. We headed down into the canopy of trees that followed the creek bed. It wasn't possible to drive a car there. And soon it wouldn't be possible to be followed even in an all terrain vehicle.

The cop on the northern corner of Front Street, who was closest to the incident at the Pathfinder, hadn't been in a position to clearly see the incident with the militia. Still, we had blasted past him immediately afterwards, so I guess he decided we had to be guilty of something. Even though we had a great head start on him, he practically gave me a heart attack when I heard his siren start up. But, by the time he was fully committed to the chase, I had already veered off down the creek trail. He probably hadn't seen me turn. He didn't even hesitate—I heard him racing off along the road that would, nevertheless, eventually intercept us. He may have thought he was chasing me. He may have known I took the pathway to the creek. Either way, his route was limited to the street and he took it. I assumed that he was also calling it in.

The bike was a late seventies Honda 350 XR or XL, adjusted somewhat for the street and the delivery work the kid did. There was a little windshield, passenger foot pegs, some kind of GPS attached to the handle bars and a rear-mounted bulky insulated container for food.

It had La Mesa written on it with the phone number. We weren't going to get far on it.

"Nance, I have an idea. I think we should head back. Go back to the restaurant. Return the bike. Grab the Pathfinder. It makes sense."

"What the hell are you saying? The place is going to be crawling with cops. They'll have called an ambulance. We can't go back. Just keep going."

"Listen, I know this bike. I had a smaller version years ago. It won't go a hundred miles without needing a fill-up and my guess is that the tank's not totally full now. Secondly, this is the Pacific Northwest. Winter. You know what that means—rain and more rain. Maybe even snow if we get unlucky. We'll freeze on this bike if we don't crash first."

"I don't care. I don't want to go back. You're insane."

"Think about it. Nobody knows exactly what we look like except maybe the FBI. And, on the street, we look like any old American couple. Secondly, we need a car, not a bike. I say we go back and look. We can *sneak* back."

"How are we going to *sneak* back?"

"This green space has lots of trails. People walk their dogs here. Kids ride their bikes. I'll head back, but try to find a different exit point. As long as we're within a block or so of the restaurant we're good. I can walk back to Front Street and suss out the situation. I'm guessing that the second cop, from the other end of the street, is there asking questions. He may be a problem. Other than him, there isn't anyone else. The militia guys are wrecked. Probably on the way to hospital as we speak. If any of their buddies showed up they're probably with them. Seriously, who else is there?"

We'd been riding for about fifteen minutes. The area was huge. The cops might have known the general vicinity of where we were, but they wouldn't have had a chance to mobilize a major search yet. The first cop who chased us might still be thinking we were ahead of him on the road. It made sense to go where they least expected. Nancy finally agreed.

We climbed a few trails that ended in fences or gates into backyards. Trespassing would only have attracted attention so we doubled back each time. I was getting a bit nervous but the area had already been shown to have public access. There must be another exit somewhere.

I was almost back at the point where we first entered the field. I was looking at taking the same path out. That made me uneasy. It was then I saw what I needed. One of the lots backing onto the green belt was empty. There was no direct trail to it but I got to within a few yards and simply powered over the bushes and into the back of the lot. When we exited the property we were on a street about two blocks from where the chase had started. And no one seemed to be there to see us.

"I'm going to risk it and drive closer. This is a quiet street. I'll park by a bush. Just stay on the bike, hold it up, leave it running and I'll go check."

"You hold it up. I'll run and check. I'm faster than you."

"Okay. Take off your helmet. That's a bit of a giveaway. Walk normally. Don't run. Look all the way up and down the street. You're looking for the second cop, any MAGA or Jefferson hats and anything whatsoever of interest. I need to have an accurate mental picture."

Nancy took off.

"Don't run!"

"Don't tell me what to do. I know what I'm doing. I can run right here."

She was gone about ten minutes. It felt like two hours. I was half crazy by the time she got back.

"What took you so long?"

"First, the ambulance is there. They must finally have the guy in it. There wasn't anyone on the ground. I think they're getting ready to leave. The cop was there and he was talking to witnesses and taking notes. There was a militia guy with one of those stupid hats beside him. The militia guy and the cop seemed to be talking a lot. The Pathfinder is still there. Che is gone."

"Damn. How long does it take to attend to an accident victim? Shouldn't they be rushing him to the damn hospital or something?"

"Well, what now, Mr. Genius? We're right back in the thick of it."

"Go down the back alley. See if Rosa's car is back. If it is, the kid's there and I may have screwed up. But, if it's not there, give me a wave and I'll drive the bike down and put it back. We can't use it anyway. We may as well close off that thread of our trail."

Nance checked. She gave me the sign to come. Rosa's car was still gone. We had caught a break. I parked the bike, took the two helmets and put them just inside the restaurant's back door. The kid might notice his bike and helmets were moved, but at least there would only be questions. I tried to park it as I found it but figured he'd notice even a slight change, as guys do. Nance and I continued up the alley along the route I had first ridden when this recent madness had begun.

"I admit that I'd hoped that the cops and everyone had dispersed by now, but the theory is still right. Hungry?"

"What?"

"Well, I'd prefer to eat at Rosa's, but there are a few other restaurants on the block. We'll go to one where we can sit by the window and watch the cop. If he leaves before a tow truck arrives, we leave. It's brilliant. And I'm hungry. What do you think?"

"Once again, I think you're insane."

206

CHAPTER FIFTY-SIX — *Charlie*

The cop was still there when the tow truck driver arrived. I was disappointed. I wasn't feeling optimistic about stealing another car since I didn't have Dale around to hotwire it for me. But then the cop left and, after a quick look inside the truck and under it, so did the tow truck driver. The Pathfinder was left sitting there.

"I think they decided that, because the truck was boxed in front and back, the tow truck driver should come back later. I guess he doesn't have the equipment to get it out sideways."

We paid, walked casually enough so as not to draw attention to ourselves, and crossed to the other side of the street.

"It's locked. Keep walking."

"Damn. I guess they had to do that, but how the hell do we get in, now?"

"Let's find a clothing store or second hand store or even a construction site. I can twist a length of wire or a coat hanger and get in."

Twenty minutes later we were in and had the car started. I pulled out slowly and carefully. No problem. Since all was going well, I turned the corner, stopped at the local gas station and filled up.

"You're pretty calm about all this, honey."

"Not on the inside. But I'm glad you're impressed."

"But, now what? Won't we be spotted?"

"Yes. I think we will. Better to get on the freeway now, I think. Hopefully they're still looking for a motorcycle and that might mean fewer cops on the freeway. But I think we stop at the first hardware store we see and get some paint and brushes."

"If you see another Pathfinder, stop. I'll swap the plates."

I was about to get on the freeway when Nancy spotted a black Pathfinder with the same body style as the one we were driving. "Follow it. There's a woman driving. Looks like she might be going shopping at that mall."

The woman pulled into a spot near Fred Meyers and took a cart from the lot. We drove down the same lane and parked a few spots south. Nance finished switching the plates in less than five minutes.

"Charlie, the problem is our plates are from California. Hers are Oregon. She may notice."

"Would you?"

"I would after this trip."

We stopped in the next mall over and picked up a couple of quarts of high gloss epoxy paint, a few brushes and other bits and pieces at the Home Depot.

"Let's head to the coast. Remember Kevin from the Mother Earth forum? We visited him some time back. Good guy. He lives near the coast. We can drop in, maybe use his garage, paint the car and then head up through Astoria."

"Kevin's politics are pretty extreme, Charlie. He could easily be a separatist. He's definitely a conspiracy theorist. You sure you want to go there?"

"Kev's wife is Thai, so he's no bigot. A lot of his paranoid theories have played out to be true, as far as I'm concerned. Think about it, he's a prepper expecting anarchy and chaos. Stores food in barrels has guns, lives remote. That should be the kind of guy we want to be in touch with."

"Yeah, but he's a flag waving patriot. Who likes to shoot. I'll bet you anything, he has a MAGA hat."

"I'll take that bet."

We drove out on the same road we had last traveled ten years earlier when we had met Kevin in person. He and I initially met on a back to the land forum and we'd seemed sympatico enough that, when Nance and I had snow-birded that year, we stopped in to visit. We really didn't know him at all well, but the visit confirmed my internet impression and we'd remained in touch over the years.

About fifteen miles in from the coast the narrow country road changed to dirt and gravel. Two miles farther a cluster of small buildings appeared, most of them surrounded by a high wood fence. I pulled up and set a pack of large dogs into a frenzy.

I'm not afraid of dogs. And barking dogs don't change that. But huge barking dogs, baring their teeth and lunging at the fence, made me hesitate. I stood at the gate deciding, once again, that discretion was a trait worth exercising.

"Who's there? State your business."

"Kev. Relax. It's Charlie and Nancy. The Canadians. You remember us, right? We occasionally talk on the forum. I guess I should have called before showing up."

Kev's tone immediately changed. Through the screened front door I saw him put his shotgun down. Then he called all the dogs to him, gave them instructions and pushed a few away. And then he opened the gate wide. Kev was smiling and extended his hand.

I accepted his hand but watched the dogs. They seemed relaxed so I stepped inside and we made the typical greetings. Nancy followed right behind me.

Nancy is more wary of dogs than I am, but once they are determined to be friendly, she's all over them. Three Rottweilers, a German Shepherd and a smaller mongrel had just met their new best friend. I was just as happy to keep my relationship with them on a more formal basis. We had tea and chatted politely for a while before I briefed Kevin on our predicament.

"So, that's it, Kev. We're on the lam. We have the FBI chasing us. We're innocent but they don't think so. If you help us they'll suspect you as well. You could be charged as an accomplice. If you choose not to get involved, Kev, we completely understand. If that's the case, all we ask is that you don't mention that we dropped by."

"What do you want?"

"A place to wash the truck, paint it and let it dry. That's it."

"It'll look painted."

"It will to someone looking at it stopped, but going sixty miles an hour it'll look like all the others."

"If we do it carefully, it might look good enough."

"We? Does that mean you're okay with this?"

"Of course. I don't know what you're accused of and I don't want you to tell me. If they ever question me, I'll just say that I knew the truck was stolen but I believed your story."

"What story?"

"The one we make up while we're painting. I'll take a few things out of the shop to make room. We can wash the truck outside and then you can pull it in and we'll get to work."

Six hours later we had washed it, wiped it down with some solvent and Kev and I had applied one coat of black paint that looked kind of plastic-y. It didn't look like the Nissan Super Black—more like a less-than-super black with some brush strokes showing.

Nancy is the detail person and went around with a solvent-soaked rag and made sure drips and splatters were cleaned up. She also climbed up and painted the roof. She cleaned all the rubber and vinyl and then put Armor All on it. The car didn't look perfect but it didn't look too bad and it definitely didn't look like it had before.

"I like it."

"Well, Kev, it doesn't look like a great paint job, does it?"

"No. But it will tomorrow."

"Why's that?"

"I'll leave some heaters on tonight. With luck it'll dry enough so that we can cut polish it tomorrow afternoon and try to get any obvious streaks out. If we do that, we can put on some wax. That'll give it some shine."

"Kev, you've been terrific. But, unfortunately, I think the poor paint job is going to be noticeable."

"True. But, like you said, maybe not at sixty miles an hour."

We stayed the night, lightly cut-polished the paint job the next day and waxed it. Amazingly, it actually didn't look all that bad. The plan was to stay another night, but it occurred to me that the quality of the paint job was less critical at night and so we decided to leave right after dinner. It was dusk when we left and when I topped up the tank in Astoria no one gave us a second look.

"The worst might be over, Nance. The FBI had a full court press going on but they won't be looking for this car. It's adequately disguised and no one knows exactly what we look like. Only the plates give us away and, with luck, the woman we took them from hasn't even noticed yet."

"Don't be silly. It's been two days. She's noticed. Or her husband has. Someone probably has. Maybe we should swap 'em out again."

"Yeah. If you see a likely swap, let me know. Ideally the car would be at an auto repair shop or another airport. We could head over to Sea-Tac and give the parking lot a cruise. I'm thinking we're better off going up the I-5 now. There's just so much traffic going through Seattle we may just blend in all the way to Bellingham."

"I disagree. We've been lucky on the coast so far. Let's stay here. And let's go by way of Port Townsend and catch the first commuter ferry in the morning. That puts us on Whidbey Island. All sorts of US forces there at the base. It's a bit like going where they wouldn't expect. Hiding in plain sight. Plus there are a few state parks there. We can stay in one and sleep in the car if we think we need to. No one is there in winter."

"I like it."

"Let's stay on the road going up Whidbey and get to Anacortes. It's all back road kinda stuff and it'll be early in the morning. Black car. We're practically invisible."

"You're thinking stealth, you know that? You're a grey panther. "

"Better than being a grey cougar."

* * * * *

"Hey, Ben. We're on our way home. As you know, we got into a bit of trouble down here so Mom and I are headed to Vancouver. We have to explain to the government about some stuff that happened. We may have to talk to the RCMP. But, basically no worries. Just a misunderstanding. But you know bureaucracy, eh? Better to be explaining to the US Homeland Security nut-bars from the safety of Canadian soil. Anyway, we'll be in touch. Hope to see you soon."

"I don't like the sound of that, Dad, so keep us informed, all right?"

"Okay. Love to you and Katie."

Five minutes later I phoned him on his burner phone.

"We've gotten away by the skin of our teeth a few times now, Ben. The FBI is close on our heels. Can you please be ready to move soon. We'll need Katie, too. We won't be able to give you much notice."

"No worries, Dad. Whatever you need."

"We'll be in touch."

212

CHAPTER FIFTY-EIGHT

Agent Henry sat at the desk assigned to him by the Portland FBI. The office was not totally unfamiliar to him. He had worked the Harding case back in '94 and '95 when the figure skater, Nancy Kerrigan, was attacked by a thug hired by Kerrigan's competitor, Tonya Harding. Henry's work on the case had not gone unnoticed and he had risen progressively through the agency since then. That career path was not looking so good right now.

"Sir, they got away. Again."

"I think I know how they did it. Ingenious."

"How?"

"We know they dropped the girl with her aunt and doubled back into Woodburn to get the Pathfinder. What we didn't know was where the motorcycle and helmets came from. Mrs. Perez did not offer that up. She should have. One of her staff has a motorcycle that answers the description. The suspects took it, ran for a bit and then doubled back. The tow truck driver couldn't easily access the stolen vehicle because of how it was parked. He and the cop left it for pick up later on. And they locked it, as per procedure. As soon as they left the couple calmly walked over, broke in like they were pros, and drove off. That's amazing. Both for their brazenness and our incompetence."

"Sir, one of the police officers did follow them when they were on the motorcycle, but lost them. The other officer had suspects and witnesses to question. Our team was not aware of the incident with the two vigilantes until after it occurred. Plus the suspects presumably had motorcycle helmets on for part of the time so they were not necessarily recognizable."

"I know. But we had six cars in a four block radius. Two old people, in a vehicle we'd already identified, drop off their passenger and leave. They delivered a teenage girl and a dog, Washington, and then up and left. We look like idiots."

"They are cool runners, sir. I'll give 'em that."

"So, anything on the Pathfinder?"

"We have a bad video of what looks like the subject vehicle filling up at a nearby gas station around the time we estimate would have been their final departure, sir. It's not particularly helpful, but it does suggest they may have headed for the I-5. Nothing since then."

"They're going north. They weren't using the Interstate before, but they may be on it now. They have enough fuel to get to the border. There are more than a few ways to cross the border, but I suspect that they'll get closer before stealing horses, sprouting wings or something equally as creative. Let's assume they have to at least get close to Bellingham before ditching the car. We're going to Burlington. It's a crossroads. Send a car to Sedro-Woolley in case they take the 9 instead of the 5."

"Sir, I suggest we have a vehicle at the Memorial-Avon junction, too, in case they head for Anacortes and turn at Mt. Vernon."

"Right. And let's get a move on. They have a few hours on us again."

* * * * *

"Sir, we have cars at the designated points. You and I have been in the chopper several times. Local police have nothing and neither has the Washington State Patrol. They've gone to ground again."

"How can they be invisible? What am I missing, Washington?"

"Sir, they may not have gone up the I-5. They've shown a preference for the coast. They may have hit the 101 again."

214

"But why? They had a head start. They're obviously not stupid. There was a good chance they could have made it through to Bellingham before we got there. Why not take the shortest and fastest route?"

"Because they know the Seattle Tacoma gridlock would slow them down? Because they're almost in their local area now that they're this far north and they know the back roads? Because they're old and need to rest?"

"Maybe. But I suspect they have friends. Or possibly acquaintances. I think they know someone here. Is there anything in their background to suggest that?"

"No, sir, not really. They don't have much of a presence in the States, except in Arizona, and a history of some RV travel over the years."

"Would you circle back to Woodburn and stay at a bed and breakfast next door to the police station? Or would you, like a normal fugitive, head up through Portland and get a few miles under your belt before calling it a day? And, if you did that, where would you sleep? In the car? My guess is that they're somewhere between Portland and Seattle, but not on the highway. If they're not at a friend's they're staying at a bed and breakfast and paying cash. Maybe a motel. But B&Bs are often located off the main streets. Easier to hide the vehicle."

"Sir, we have a list of B&Bs in Washington State. There are approximately two hundred. If we just look at the area between here and Bellingham and eliminate the eastern half of the state, I think it might be down to about a hundred. Do you want us to contact them?"

"Yes. We can't physically cover the territory. Get a phone crew on it. Keep the inquiries discreet. Just mention a stolen car."

"And our cars on the highway?"

"Keep the rotations going for a bit longer. If they have gone to ground, they may have done so in anticipation of us dropping the highway surveillance. Let's keep it in place for now."

* * * * *

"Sir, we have nothing. The intercept teams have been working 'round the clock."

"So, Washington, what are you saying? You think we pull them?"

"I think it's good that it's your decision and not mine."

"Well, I'm leaving them in place until midnight. After that, ask local police to do what they can. I'm going to concentrate on Anacortes. If I were them, I'd walk on the ferry."

"*Anacortes?* Why do you think that?"

"Firstly, they know both Vancouver and Victoria equally well. Vancouver is not a given. Secondly, they obviously can't take the car through the border or on the ferry with stolen plates, not to mention the car itself being stolen. They wouldn't risk driving it across the border. So, how do they walk across the border? They don't. They float across."

"Canada allows a lot of so-called refugees to simply walk across the border. Why wouldn't they just go with the crowd?"

"Right. Problem is it isn't a crowd. There were only about a thousand refugees who went into British Columbia last year. That's a steady stream, but no more than three or four a day. The most people they could possibly have to blend in with would maybe be a family. And many of them are going to be Hispanic, although apparently BC does get quite a few from Iraq and the Middle East, too. We've asked the Canada Border Services Agency to look for our couple and, if spotted, hold them until the Royal Canadian Mounted Police arrive. The RCMP has agreed to hand them over to us. They take murder charges seriously."

216

"Do they know the circumstances? Do they know the Canadians will plead self defense?"

"I bet they get people trying to talk their way out of everything, just as much as we do. They'll hand them over."

"What do you want done in Anacortes then, sir?"

"Well, have a car at the entrance to town. I want that Pathfinder spotted. These people have avoided the police so far, so don't use the local force in town. Unmarked cars only. They're not afraid to lay low for awhile so that means they may ditch the car somewhere. The local cops can at least keep watch for the Pathfinder. Contact all the car rental, taxi and limo services to report any older people hiring a car to the ferry. Have all the hotels and motels, and as many B&Bs as possible, report anyone meeting our profile. Don't panic anyone. Keep it low key. You can get us set up in a hotel, or a Federal government facility if there is one, as soon as possible. They could already be there if they caught a break in traffic."

"Sir?"

"What?"

"Are we not betting all our chips on this one horse?"

"Mixed metaphor, Washington, but yes. And I appreciate your observation. Put a car at the Douglas Border Crossing and the one east of that—the Pacific Highway Truck Crossing. I'm going to risk not placing a car at Sumas because pedestrians can't easily cross there, but make sure the Canada Border Services is especially vigilant at that location. That is the one place I wouldn't expect them to go and, as you know, they've done the unexpected before."

"Yes, sir, and I'm getting us set up at The Tall Ship Inn in Anacortes, right now. Right beside the ferry terminal and two minutes from the airport. It's fairly basic, but relatively vacant this time of year. They even gave us a forty percent discount."

"The Agency values parsimony, Washington."

"Thank you, sir. I know you are aware, that with the placement of most of our teams elsewhere, there are just two cars, in addition to us, in Anacortes."

"How many agents do you think we need to take down two senior citizens?"

"You know Nance, Anacortes is a big risk. It's the most likely spot for us to jump the border. The FBI isn't stupid. Maybe we should go east to Idaho and cross into Alberta or something."

"I'm willing to do that if you think it's best, but I'm tired of running. And there's no indication the FBI even knows we're in Washington State yet."

"Have you checked messages?"

"I'd better do that. Oh, no. I have a text from Dale. He said the FBI is up to speed on us. They went to Woodburn. The head agent is a guy called Henry. Older guy. Black partner called Washington. Dale had to talk to protect Ana. He's very, very sorry."

"Well, that explains the two local cops on Front Street. We probably missed some FBI agents by not going to the house. I bet they arrived late or staked out Rosa's house. They were much closer than we thought."

"And you thought stopping for dinner was such a great idea."

"We got lucky. We have more than once, I might add. So what do you think about taking the ferry from Anacortes to Sidney?"

"Your call. You've been calling it right so far. But, if it was left to me, I'd go now. As fast as we can to keep one step ahead of them. The FBI isn't perfect. The car is a different color now. I think it's a timing thing and we currently have time on our side. The more time we take to make the leap across the border, the more time they'll have to alert border services and get organized."

"Yeah, you're right. We can't take the car over the border and almost all the crossings pretty much require us to have a vehicle. The more easterly we go, the more snow there's going to be, too. Okay, that settles it. The ferry it is."

"Charlie, I suggest we take a water taxi to Friday Harbor and then board the ferry there."

"Well, I suppose. But wouldn't we stand out more in a small place like Friday Harbor? I mean, getting on the ferry there, wouldn't we be the only ones?"

"You think it's safer boarding in Anacortes?"

"I do. More cars. More people. But only if we board by car with Katie. Walking on would be as open and exposed as walking on at Friday Harbor."

"But that means Katie has to come all the way to Anacortes and stay the night. Plus we'd all be seen together. Wouldn't that implicate her?"

"If it comes to that, we simply have to say we asked her to come and, like a good daughter-in-law, she did. And we all have to stick to that. And I doubt very much that they would try and prosecute her. She really doesn't know why they're chasing us, only that we didn't get our papers processed right. Let's leave it at that."

"I wish we could get on without using her."

"Her car is licensed and registered in her name. No alarms will go off with it because it's a different last name. The only risk is that we'll be in it. But she has an excuse for that. The hammer will fall on us only, and even that possibility is reduced a great deal by being in her car, rather than anything else."

"I have an idea. Ask her to go to Friday Harbor. We'll take a water taxi from Anacortes to Friday Harbor. The next day we walk onto the ferry at Friday Harbor. She drives on. We still won't have been seen with her. And she doesn't even have to be seen in public with us until the last second before we arrive in Sidney."

"Good thinking. I'll tell Ben. I'll ask him to have Katie book a large suite at the Friday Harbor Lodge. Enough room for the three of us. It's a five minute walk to the ferry terminal. We'll get on the ferry separately."

* * * * *

"Ben, we're going to cross into Canada at the Douglas Border Crossing. We'll be coming by bus. That should give us a bit of a crowd to mingle with. We'll come in on a Sunday, too. It'll be busy. We may sit separately, to look as inconspicuous as possible. The bus will drop us off downtown."

"Okay. Call me when you can. I'll come and pick you up in Vancouver."

Five minutes later I called Ben on the burner phone: "We're actually coming by way of the Anacortes ferry to Sidney. Please get Katie to catch the 12:05 ferry from Sidney tomorrow and get off in Friday Harbor. Ask her to reserve a return trip on the ferry to Sidney at 9:55 the next day. If anyone asks, she's coming to pick up her in-laws as we requested. She has no idea we are wanted for anything but immigration issues. She just came to get us because we had to leave the rental car in the US and my knee was acting up, making walking difficult."

"Okay. So, let's be clear. She knows nothing except that you had a rental car after the pickup truck broke down in Barstow. That's it. Nothing more. I'll tell her I had to go to Vancouver for motorcycle parts. And I *will* go. But if this blows up, it'll look like I'm an accomplice going to Vancouver to mislead them. They'll have that from the phone call, if they're monitoring."

"You're right. That would look bad for you. How about you start out for Vancouver and decide that you can't go through with it, even though you wanted to do as I asked. You call Katie to say you'll go with her. But she turned her phone off. Nance always does. It's plausible. You can figure that out. That means you initially had the intent but changed your mind."

"I'm not sure if that'd hold up. But I don't care. If they get you and you end up in Guantanamo or Sing Sing, I can claim I had no idea what you'd done and simply wanted to be a good son. I may get charged but I doubt I'd go to prison. It's you guys who are the ones at risk."

"We do think that Anacortes is a risk. We could go east to some border crossing way off the radar but, unless they spot us with facial recognition patterns, the only real risk is if they have FBI agents at the Sidney ferry dock. I think that's the key issue. I don't know if the FBI has powers in Canada."

"They do. They call it Integrated Border-something. It allows the police from either side to act with disregard for the border within fifty miles of it. FBI guys can arrest you in Canada. I suppose RCMP guys can arrest someone in the USA but *that's* not likely to happen."

"Okay. In that case, you remember my friend in Vancouver, John Burgoyne? He's at the Burgoyne, Burgoyne and Burgoyne law firm downtown. They do cross border business deals. Probably represent a lot of American interests. Call John. Tell him what's going on, after insisting he take a dollar IOU, which gives us client confidentiality. You have to do that. If he doesn't agree to have his firm take this on, ask him to give you the name of someone in another law firm that specializes in Immigration or Criminal law."

"What good will that do?"

"I only care that, if we're arrested, we get arrested by the RCMP and we stay in Canada. I can't have those bastards handing us over to the Feds. We can't go back to the US. Their system is worse than ours."

"Okay. I'll find somebody if John can't do it."

"Oh, I don't think he'll do it himself. But he can get a lawyer in his firm to. John's specialty is corporate law. He'll refer us to someone who'll make waves with the RCMP."

"Okay. Got it."

* * * * *

The water taxi dropped us off at the Friday Harbor marina around nine. The picturesque little seaport was to be our hideaway for the next twenty four hours. Our hotel was a few blocks away. It would have been romantic if it wasn't so early in the morning and raining.

"Should we walk?"

"It's only a few blocks but I hate being in the open right now. I confess to feeling more vulnerable without our poorly painted stolen car with illegal plates. Weird, eh?"

"No. I feel the same way. My suggestion is we walk half way and stop at the nearest coffee shop to have breakfast and suss things out."

"I'm in favor of breakfast but there's not much to suss out now. We're here. For better or worse. I say we get to the hotel after eating and hunker down there until it's time to leave in the morning."

"Deal."

"Maybe stop for a bottle of wine."

"Deal."

"Pizza for dinner? Delivered?"

"Sounds good."

"Déjà vu, sweetie."

"What do you mean?"

"Our third date, fifty years ago. Same pizza and wine seduction ploy. You fell for it again."

"Hard to resist that kind of charm."

CHAPTER SIXTY

"Sir, we've intercepted a call to the son. Apparently the suspects are planning on catching a bus and crossing at Douglas. They think a busload of people will give them some cover."

"That's good news. Too good, actually. Still, send the unit to Blaine. You and I will stay here."

"Why? Just to be sure?"

"You could say that. If they walk across at either the Douglas Crossing or the truck crossing, we'll get them. But, anyway, I don't believe they're actually heading there."

"Why not?"

"These people have been pretty elusive. They have their wits about them. They're not so stupid as to go there. I think it's a red herring."

"Think the kid's in on it?"

"Doubt it. The old guy probably wouldn't want to involve the kid except to feed him false information. Maybe he suspects we tapped the kid's phone. I would if I were him. So far he's been thinking like us, only quicker, unfortunately. I think the Douglas crossing is the least likely place for them to go."

"Should we reassign that team?"

"Washington. You're killing me, here. The only intel we have is that they're going through the Douglas Crossing. If we ignore that and they actually do use it, my head will roll. Your career will be mothballed. They'll talk about that mistake at Quantico for years to come. We have to cover our butts. Comes with the job."

"So, it is just you and me in Anacortes?

"You have a problem with that, Washington?"

"Not at all, sir."

"Tell me, Washington, why did you join the FBI?"

"I had just graduated law school. Not a lot of firms wanted me. The FBI did. They recruited me."

"But you agreed. Why?"

"I suppose for all the reasons you'd think. Service, duty, heroism, adventure, good pay, respect. I like wearing a suit. But it was more than that, really. As you may have noticed, I'm black. This is a racist country. I think I can help fix that more by working within the system than from without. Why?"

"I was just thinking back to when I signed up twenty-five years ago. And, to be honest, I can't remember why I did. I remember that I was recruited, too. After the army. I think I joined simply because I had no other plans. But I do know that I always looked up to the FBI. Always had respect for the institution."

"And now?"

"That's the real question, isn't it? The president doesn't think much of the FBI right now. But I do. The administration thinks highly of ICE. And I do not. That is strictly between you and me, you understand. I'm just wondering about my place in all of this, that's all. Maybe it's just age. I'm past fifty. People have mid-life crises, Washington. Maybe this is mine."

"I don't think so, sir. A lot of us are thinking this way. I certainly am. If the country has no faith in us, why should we?"

"Because we're doing the right thing?"

"That's the second big question, sir. Are we?"

* * * * *

"Agent Henry, according to the Victoria Police Department the son left the house. They added something that makes no sense."

"What's that?"

"His wife also left the house at the same time in her car."

"So?"

"They both went to Sidney. The terminal for the ferry to Anacortes is there but so is the terminal for the Vancouver ferry."

"So, what did the Victoria Police conclude from that?"

"VPD is just reporting in to us. I don't think they're trying to make any sense of it. I don't know what information their commander gave them. But they reported both vehicles leaving and so took the initiative and followed them. When the suspects got to Sidney, the son went to the ferry terminal to go to Vancouver, as expected. They didn't follow him because they knew where he was going."

"So far, there's no story here . . . unless the daughter-in-law is going to Anacortes. What ferry is she on?"

"She has a reservation for the 12:05 p.m. That means she arrives in Anacortes at three o'clock. Your hunch may have been right. Should we detain her?"

"No. Let her get the couple first. We'll pick them up on our side of the border."

* * * * *

"Sir, we've confirmed the daughter-in-law got off at Friday Harbor. She must be staying somewhere in the village."

"Damn. The old couple must have taken a water taxi there. We're still playing catch up. Get the chopper. Book us a place to stay in Friday Harbor."

I was in the upper lounge of the ferry trying to look invisible. What struck me as amusing was that the FBI guys across the room were doing just the opposite. They couldn't have been more obvious. After I watched them for a few minutes, the younger guy got up and left.

I knew it was a gamble, but I wanted to meet the guy chasing me. Maybe I could find a way to dissuade him. It was a long shot but worth taking, I figured. I was virtually unrecognizable from my passport photo. I'd shaven my face clean, lost twenty pounds and my hair was quite a bit longer. Plus I was wearing my reading glasses.

"Pardon me. I apologize for the intrusion, but would you mind if I asked you a question?"

Agent Henry looked up at the stocky older gentleman and said, "How can I help you?"

"It may sound odd, but I try to profile people. I'm an author and I try to write my characters based on real people I meet. I've been trying to come up with a law enforcement type, FBI kinda guy. I was just over there thinking about it when I saw you and your colleague. And I watched your interaction. Please don't take offense, but I thought you two were acting like perfect detectives, FBI guys, or at least some kind of non-uniformed police. Am I close?"

"Please, sit down. I'm Patrick Henry and you are?"

"Trevor Stickler. You may have read one of my books. I write about the San Juan Islands, but mostly the live-aboard community. People who live on boats."

"No, Mr. Stickler, I'm sorry. I haven't read your books. I'm sure I'd enjoy them."

"The last one is called 'Natural Hy'. It's pretty good and I really enjoyed writing the story. It was wonderfully cathartic for me. But Mr. Henry, did I guess wrong?"

"No, sir. You did not. I do work for the government. That was my partner. I have to ask you what gave us away."

"Well, for fear of being stereotypical, both of you are of working age. It's a weekday so it's likely you're working. You're both wearing good suits. Not great ones. No vanity there. You could be salesmen but you're traveling to Canada and you're Americans, so that would be unlikely. Plus, your manner on the ferry is one steeped in work ethic. You guys are not just having a boat ride. And there's more."

"Please. I'm curious."

"Well, you are the superior. You guys are not equals on the job. He does what you tell him. That was easy. You're both fit and yet *you* are, forgive me, getting on a bit. I'm guessing fifty-five. So, you work out. He does, too."

"Anything else?"

"Yes. You both scanned the room. I'm guessing more than once. I didn't notice right away, but you scanned it once when I did notice, and then again just before I ventured over. Who does that on a ferry? It's not likely you're expecting anyone. So, you're extremely watchful. It's intriguing. Especially since I got it right."

"I'm impressed."

"Thanks. But you can give the credit to Conan Doyle."

"Who?"

"Sir Arthur Conan Doyle. He wrote the Sherlock Holmes stories. I try to throw a little of that observation and deduction into my stories as well. Not like Doyle, of course. Too much of that kind of thing doesn't go over so well with readers today."

"So what do modern readers want?"

"I don't really know. I'm not a best seller. But, according to Lee Child's formula, they want a fast pace, short bursts of action, and a quick read that requires no complicated vocabulary or complex sentence structure. The modern reader has a short attention span. Probably as a result of the last few generations being raised on television."

"You're interesting, Mr. Stickler. I may pick up one of your books. I'm glad you sat down."

"Thank you. A polite person would interpret that as you saying I may be excused and so I shall take my leave but, I would like to ask you about your name before I go. Patrick Henry is the patriot who famously said, 'Give me liberty or give me death.'"

"I know. I'm a distant relative. My parents wanted to keep the name in the family. Actually, I prefer being called Agent Henry."

"At the risk of overstaying my welcome, Agent Henry, I'll ask if there is not, sometimes, a little dissonance at work inside of you. Your name and the famous quote infer one thing, and yet you apprehend people, depriving them of their liberty."

"Only those who deserve it, Mr. Stickler. And all in aid of keeping peaceful people free. That is the order of the day."

"Did you quote him on purpose, Agent Henry?"

"Quote who?"

"Lieutenant William Calley. That's what he said at his trial for massacring innocent people at My Lai."

I didn't smile. I just looked at him. And then I turned and left. I could feel Henry's eyes on my receding back.

CHAPTER SIXTY-TWO

"Washington, I think I may have met our guy."

"Really, sir? Where?"

"Right here. He came over and chatted with me. Said his name was Stickler. Claimed to be an author. But I think it was him. Something tells me it's the guy we're looking for."

"Did he look like his picture?"

"Yeah. Somewhat. Clean shaven, though. Wearing glasses. But the right age, I think. Same hair cut, a bit longer. White dress shirt and jeans. I wouldn't say I was one hundred percent sure, but the feeling was there. Trouble is he looks just like a lot of guys."

"You want to go find him?"

"No. Where's he going to go? We have the RCMP setting up at Sidney. There's plenty of them and only two of us. No need to make a scene. They can pick him up. Have you spotted the daughter-in-law?"

"No. I spotted the car but we have no picture of her yet. Young woman in her early thirties. But, like you said, where can she go? She gets in her car, they stop her at the border and we walk up ten minutes later."

"They're not stopping her at the border are they?"

"Not to make the arrest. Just to make sure it's the suspects we're looking for. Then they'll be stopped a block down the road that exits the terminal. The RCMP suggested this would be easier than trying to arrest them right at the customs booths. Too much traffic there. Too many people. This way is much safer for everyone."

"Good. I'll be more than a little surprised if it's not the guy who introduced himself to me."

"Why would he do that?"

"I don't know. It wasn't only risky but nothing was gained except he now knows for sure that we're here. He likely knows his time is up. But he's not going to do anything crazy. I have to say I enjoyed speaking with him. He's sane. Made me think."

"About what?"

"Oh, about what we do and why we do it. How you and I look working together. He shared some observations. But I suspect he had more than just a hunch to go on. Still, you and I need to get new suits."

"He dissed our suits? My suit's great but I'll gladly help you pick out a nice ensemble anytime. Just say the word. Let's start with the tie first, as soon as possible. By the way, did you see the woman?"

"No. But that makes sense. If he suspected we were FBI then there is no logic for them to sit together. As it is, I'm still not sure my author was him. He certainly played me if it *was* him. I just don't know."

"So, where's the woman?"

"Maybe she connected with the daughter-in-law. Maybe she got the key and is sitting in the car. Doesn't matter. She's on this boat somewhere. The net is closing. And what the hell is wrong with my tie?"

CHAPTER SIXTY-THREE — *Charlie*

"So, Charlie, how is this all going to work when we get to Sidney?"

"I'm going to get Katie to stop at customs, whether they instruct us to or not."

"Okay, that's a start."

"Ben will pick up John from the Vancouver ferry. John will be wearing jeans and a white shirt. The plan requires that John and I dress alike but, of course, John doesn't know that."

"That sounds a little nuts."

"That's not even the nutty part. Your sister, Mary, will drive out to Sidney and meet up with Ben and John before our ferry arrives. They will all be in Ben's Astro Van when he comes to the customs office. Mary's hair is white like yours and we'll ask her to dress in a white top and jeans as well. You know Mary, she won't even ask why. She'll only know that we asked her to come and support you in case you get arrested."

"You think you can fool a bunch of cops?"

"Not really. The odds are slim, but think of it this way, what have we got to lose? If they arrest us at the customs office, there's no risk to anyone we've involved. No one has done anything wrong. If they don't arrest us at the office—and I don't think they will because we're classified as armed and dangerous and there are far too many staff and public milling about—we'll go back to the car. By then both vehicles will be in the parking lot. We'll discreetly get into the other vehicle."

"They'll see us."

"Maybe, but John is close to my age and build. We cut a similar figure, as do you and Mary. And I have Ben parking in the spot closest to the building. That will block the view of Katie's car somewhat. I'll instruct Katie to park as close to him as possible and use his car to block the view of her car from the office windows. When she pulls in, we all get out and enter the building. All eyes will be on us. Mary slips into the back seat of Katie's car at that point."

"What about John? Won't he be regarded as complicit if you pull this off?"

"No. He has plausible deniability. When Katie pulls in with us, he remains in the van for a few seconds and then gets out and follows us into the office. But, before he introduces himself, he goes to the washroom. So does Ben. I'll borrow Katie' phone and John and I will have an open line. If we're arrested at that point, I simply speak into the phone and ask him to come right away.

"If we're let go to be arrested a few minutes later down the road, then we go out to Katie's car, put our luggage in it and she gets in. We then slip into Ben's van. Ben leaves John in the customs office and drives out with us hidden in the backseat. Nothing about that is illegal because we were released."

"What about John?"

"John comes out last, gets into Katie's car and they, with Mary who is already there, leave in the target vehicle. They don't look exactly like us but, if the roadblock is manned by local RCMP, the cops won't know. They have descriptions of us, which John and Mary generally fit, but they will be mostly focused on the car. If we don't get away, then no one did anything wrong. We're allowed to ride with family. We're allowed to switch cars. No laws broken. No one is complicit."

"It's a long shot."

"I know. But nothing is risked. If we're arrested at the customs office, John is there to help us. If not, then we have a chance to do the bait and switch."

"CCTV cameras watch the parking area as well as officers. What if someone sees us?"

"No one watches while the cameras are recording. They're for later review. And if someone does see us, getting into our son's car is not illegal, so it won't make matters worse. If we don't do this we are caught anyway so we have nothing to lose."

"And what about Ben driving us? Won't we have to go through the roadblock?"

"Maybe. We'll have to play that by ear. If the roadblock is close to the Customs office property, then he may have to try to get through and we may get caught. But, if the roadblock is a block away, where it should be so as to avoid endangering the public, he can simply pull over to the side of the road before he reaches it and park for a few minutes."

"Why park?"

"We wait for Katie to leave the customs lot, drive down the street to the road block and get stopped. She, John and Mary will be arrested and taken back to the Customs office in handcuffs. The local RCMP will have acted on the information they had, rendered the fugitives harmless and won't even notice the van leaving the scene after they've taken their prisoners in."

"I don't think we have much of a chance."

"I agree. But, nothing ventured, nothing gained and, in this case, nothing made worse by the effort as well."

"Are you sure they won't arrest us in the office?"

"Not really, but we are considered armed and dangerous. Would they want to risk that in a place frequented with the public and their staff? Logic says they'd do it in the parking lot. But you know the Sidney Customs lot; it's really tight in there and the cars lining up for the outbound ferry trip will fill most of it. It's always really congested. Good sense suggests they set up a roadblock down the street where they can establish a clear perimeter."

"What about the FBI guys?"

"That's an unknown, but we're pretty sure they're walking off the ferry so that'll take a few minutes. They most likely won't be at the customs office when we get there. My guess is that they'll leave the arrest to the Canadian cops. Good politics. Still, they could arrive soon after and see us doing the switch and make a move."

"So, let's assume we get caught. Then what?"

"We thank God that John is there to save us from the FBI by insisting we be arrested by the RCMP and remain in Canada."

"Can John do that?"

"No idea, but if anyone can, he can. That's the biggest risk of all, though."

"So we're escaping but no one is a knowing accomplice?"

"Well, now you are. I shouldn't have told you, but you won't make a move unless I give you the whole picture."

"Damn right. I'm on a need to know everything basis, even if it means we go to the slammer together, big boy."

CHAPTER SIXTY-FOUR

"Sir, can you come with us, please?"

"Of course, officer. What seems to be the problem?"

"You are wanted, sir. The FBI has requested that the RCMP detain you. We are authorized by the Integrated Cross Border Law Enforcement Operations Act to work in concert with US authorities."

"I have no doubt you are, officer, but I'd like to know why I'm being detained. In fact, I need to hear from you that you're arresting me, and on what charge, or I won't cooperate."

"Sir, under the Act, we can detain you for any reason for seventy-two hours. I'm sorry, sir, but conventional rights do not apply in this situation."

"Fine. I accept that you have the legal authority at this time but shouldn't you be able to tell me what you suspect me of?"

"Sir, I don't know. That will be fully explained to you by the FBI, I'm sure. Their agents will be here shortly."

"I protest vehemently. I've done nothing to warrant the FBI's attention. I haven't even been to the United States in the last six months."

"Sir, I will warn you only once. I can be called as a material witness. My suggestion to you is that you shut up before you make things worse for yourself."

"Yes, officer, I will shut up, as per your instructions. But I'm protesting this unwarranted detention. Is that clear?"

"Like Windex, sir. Now shut up."

John took a seat in the RCMP cruiser and watched as Mary and Katie were escorted to a separate car. He noted the exact time and remembered the conversation with the officer as accurately as he could, which was rather well since he had a photographic memory. He smiled to himself—the officer had instructed him to be silent.

* * * * *

Agent Henry looked at the stocky older, clean-shaven man with glasses, in a white shirt and jeans, sitting in front of him. "Sir, what is your name, please?"

"John Burgoyne."

"Do you know why you're here?"

"I know why I'm here at the ferry terminal. I have no idea why I'm talking to you."

"Sir, how did you and Mary Hoffman come to be in Ms Chiu's car?"

"Before I answer that, who are you?"

"My apologies. I assumed the CBSA officers told you. My name is Henry. Agent Patrick Henry. This is my colleague, Agent Washington. We're with the FBI."

"Okay. So, why are you detaining me?"

"We're not detaining you, sir. We thought we had detained two fugitives but it would appear that the RCMP apprehended the wrong people. It would seem that you were detained in error."

"Great. Am I free to go?"

"Not quite, sir. We know that Ms Chiu gave the two fugitives a ride and she admits that she did. She arrived at this very office with them in her car. The three of them entered the office. They were questioned briefly and released. Our reason for that was simply with public safety in mind. We wanted to identify the suspects with the intention of apprehending them down the road where it would be safer, in case of resistance."

"You expected resistance?"

"We did, sir. They were reported as armed."

"So, you're asking me what? How I and Mrs. Hoffman came to be in Ms Chiu's car?"

"Exactly."

"Well, friends, and clients, of mine, asked me to come to Sidney in case they were arrested. They also asked Mrs. Hoffman. She's Mrs. Moon's sister. Mr. Moon told me that he and his wife are innocent of any charges that might be pending and that he was concerned about being apprehended. He said that the FBI might attempt to arrest them here in Canada and, if that happened, they could be returned to the US. He was extremely concerned about entering the labyrinth that is Homeland Security, ICE and the FBI, not to mention local state police and whatever other agencies might be involved. My client told me that he and his wife preferred to surrender themselves to the RCMP with legal counsel present, rather than be apprehended and whisked away by US authorities. As his lawyer, I agreed to meet him here to make sure that his and his wife's rights were respected."

"Sir, your clients have no rights. They're wanted on three counts of murder."

"Well, then, it would seem that his fears were well founded. To claim he has no rights as a Canadian citizen on Canadian soil would seem to violate the intent and wording of the Integrated Cross Border Law Enforcement Operations Act."

"That's debatable, Mr. Burgoyne. But please answer the question. How did you come to be in Ms Chiu's car?"

"Ben Moon drove me here. I went to the washroom and when I came out his wife, Katie, told me the Moons had been released and their son had taken them home. Their fears had not been realized—they hadn't been arrested. She said she'd give me a ride back to the Vancouver ferry and she thanked me for being here in case I was needed. I walked out with Katie and got in her car. That was when I met Mary Hoffman. We were stopped down the road by the RCMP."

"Did you inform them as to who you were?"

"They didn't ask who I was. In fact, they told me to shut up and wait until I was interviewed by the FBI. So, I complied."

"Mr. Burgoyne, we may have grounds to arrest you for obstruction of justice. You knowingly facilitated the escape of two suspected murderers. You knew they were being pursued and you obstructed that pursuit. I think we have a charge."

"I deny the charge. May I remind you that I admitted knowing that they were suspected of a crime and that is why I attended today. Upon learning that they had not been detained, I felt that my services were no longer required and I accepted a ride to the ferry. That is not obstruction. That is, in essence, non-participation. I might even have trouble billing for my time. Now, is there anything else before I go to see my other clients?"

"And who might they be?"

"Ms Chiu and Mrs. Hoffman. When we were stopped by the RCMP, they asked that I represent them if it was necessary. In light of the intimidation and threats I have just experienced, I deem it necessary."

"Mr. Burgoyne, we may have gotten off on the wrong foot. May I respectfully request that you stay and answer a few more questions. To make that an easier decision, I acknowledge that you did not impede justice. I also acknowledge that I mistook your role. And, finally, I will give you unimpeded access to Ms Chiu and Mrs. Hoffman. I'd just like to know a few things."

"Give me five minutes with them and I'll return to tell you what I can."

CHAPTER SIXTY-FIVE

"How are they treating you and Mary, Katie?"

"They're asking us what you'd expect. Are we in trouble?"

"No. You've done nothing wrong. Having said that, I'm now advising you both not to say anything more. Agreed?"

"Absolutely. Do you think they're going to let us go?"

"Just a matter of time."

* * * * *

"Sir, we have nothing. To be honest, I really don't think Chiu was in on it at all. I think they used them both. But neither knew the role she was playing. Each did what I would've done in their place and I see nothing else there. Maybe you should talk to them?"

"No. I trust your judgment, Washington. And it makes sense. This couple doesn't put others at risk."

"What about the lawyer?"

He knows something. He has to. What big-time lawyer takes a day off from the office to meet a friend? Maybe Moon is into something bigger? I'm going to pry a bit more, but I agree. We have nothing. I think those suspects just made our job a whole lot harder. Now, if we go after them, we have a mountain of legal paperwork to climb. And I don't think much of our chances."

"Why? We know they killed three people. We have the power to arrest in Canada. How can they get away with this?"

"Well, Washington, except for the car and boat thefts, the crimes were committed in Arizona. Canada won't allow extradition on murder charges to states with the death penalty. If they're prosecuted they'll be tried in a Canadian court. That takes forever. I'll be retired before there's a decision. And if they're convicted they'll serve their jail time in Canada. It'll basically be out of our hands."

"So, you'd consider that a hollow victory?"

"More than hollow, Washington. Deep-hole empty. We may have been beaten. It may be better to cut our losses, considerable as they are."

"And let two murderers get away scot free?"

"I admit, I'm not happy. I'm going to see what the RCMP can do for us, but I doubt that they're going to send out much in the way of manpower. Maybe a bulletin to their members or something. But are they going to mount a massive pursuit like we did? I don't think so."

* * * * *

"Mr. Burgoyne, I just want to know why the top lawyer in a large firm such as yours would drop everything and take the day off from an important practice to meet a client coming into Canada. It begs credulity."

"Not really, Agent Henry. I've known Charlie Moon for over forty years. He's always been honest and ethical—I'd trust him with my family. His son said he was running from vigilantes and was forced to defend himself. I know nothing more than that and I have no idea what defend means in this context. But I do know about the total cluster fuck that short-lived vigilante effort created in Arizona. Unleashing rabid dogs on innocent people. The stories coming out of that fiasco are unbelievable. I'm not an expert in US law, but I imagine there will be enough lawsuits flying around to keep everyone busy for a long, long time. I expect that a lot of charges will be laid and a lot of resignations will be tendered."

"It was bad. I admit that. But your clients committed real crimes."

"My clients told their son that they didn't break any laws. But the US Customs and Border Protection, not to mention ICE, have routinely defied court orders and violated US law when detaining immigrants and foreigners. In the United States today too many people are assumed guilty until proven innocent and, if you have any doubts about that statement, just look at the policies of your government agencies. In that kind of environment, would *you* voluntarily turn yourself in, Agent Henry?"

"I can't assume they're innocent. That's not my job. My job is to apprehend, not judge. I want to know what happened. I want to interview and question my suspects. We have an agreement with your country. You have to give them up."

"Ben told me that his parents would be willing to cooperate fully on the condition that it was all done in Canada. I am merely repeating that."

"And if we have hard evidence that there was a crime committed?"

"Well, in the authoritarian climate that has cast a pall over your country, it's likely that people running from persecution might break laws. We consider the vigilantism, created by the crackdown in Arizona, unlawful persecution in the extreme. So we'll vigorously defend all accusations."

"I'm talking about murder."

"So am I, Agent Henry. So am I."

* * * * *

"What happened, Mr. Burgoyne?"

"Call me, John, Katie. We've been in battle together."

"Okay, John, I know Mary and I are free to go. But what's going to happen to Charlie and Nancy?"

"Henry will have to file for their extradition. He wouldn't be doing his job if he didn't. If he files quickly and asks for little, it's a sign that he's just going through the motions to cover himself. And that's what I expect him to do.

"He has other problems on his plate right now, Katie. The US justice system is hugely compromised. Furthermore, the FBI is a dog that's being kicked by the current administration. Those guys are going to have to focus on bigger issues. I think he sees pursuing Charlie and Nancy any further as being a significant drain on the Bureau's manpower and budget. It already has been.

"But, most of all, Henry told me as much. He shook my hand when he left and while he was doing so, he said something interesting. He asked me to tell Charlie 'Doing the right thing is the order of the day.'"

Acknowledgements

Our sincerest gratitude is extended—

To our beta readers who spent an amazing amount of time giving thoughtful and badly needed feedback. You are indispensable.

Mary Boegel

Katharine and Steve Barnes (no relation to Dale)

John and Mary Caroline Hart

Rachel and Roger Mattice

Sid Midtdal

Judy Kelly and Trevor Stickler

To our daughter, Emily Robertson, who, to aid in her composition and shooting of the cover photo, borrowed a cup of bullets from a neighbor.

About the Authors

J. David Cox and Sally J. Davies live on a remote island off the coast of British Columbia and have been together for over forty years. Dave has worked with refugees, ridden motorcycles professionally, been a bouncer *and* a mediator and once painted a Volkswagen van with a brush. Sally has wasted time in a lot of meetings, stolen a dog and occasionally given the finger to annoying drivers, inadvertently involving Dave in fisticuffs. As well, they have spent a great deal of time in Mexico and listened to many stories told by undocumented migrant workers.

Dave also wrote (and Sally edited) the surprisingly popular:

OUR LIFE OFF THE GRID:
An Urban Couple Goes Feral

David and his wife Sally, in their mid-fifties, went from being white collar urbanites to living off the grid on a remote island in the wilds of west coast British Columbia, Canada. In this lighthearted memoir they face the challenges of constructing their own home by reading how-to books, adapting to an off-grid lifestyle and learning to live with the wildlife, including their few, but eccentric neighbors.

and the cult classic:

CHOOSING OFF THE GRID

"Get out! Get out now!" is J. David Cox's advice to city dwellers. If you're thinking of moving off the grid you'll learn from Dave how it feels. Sometimes practical, often philosophical, you'll read things you won't hear elsewhere. Settle back and enjoy Dave's unique, personal, and, in this book, more serious approach, to life off the grid.